PERFECTLY REASONABLE

LINDA O'CONNOR

Laugh every day.
Love every minute.
Linda

SOUL MATE PUBLISHING

New York

PERFECTLY REASONABLE

Copyright©2015

LINDA O'CONNOR

Cover Design by Rae Monet, Inc.

Published in the United States of America by
Soul Mate Publishing
P.O. Box 24
Macedon, New York, 14502

ISBN: 978-1-68291-009-2

ebook ISBN: 978-1-61935-907-9

www.SoulMatePublishing.com

Karen Marcotte ~
who handed me the beautiful journal
she had just won
and said, "Write me a story."
Here you go.

Vlad Kratky ~ I love you.

Acknowledgements

I would like to thank Debby Gilbert at Soul Mate Publishing for providing the ultimate encouragement to my writing with the leap to publishing. Huge thanks to the team at Soul Mate Publishing and to Rae Monet for the beautiful cover design.

Special thanks to my Canadian editor Ellie Barton, and to Shirley Baird, Wendy Reynolds, and Lesley Rooke – an excellent team of beta readers!

Thank you from my heart to:

Vlad, for sharing this journey with me (even though romance is not your genre :D),

Brad, Tom, and Mark, who answer all my research questions and never complain about leftovers,

my mom, for all of her wonderful advice,

Karen, artist of beautiful cards and my most avid supporter, and everyone who read Perfectly Honest and encouraged me along the way.

Here you have it – Perfectly Reasonable – another dream come true!

Dear Reader,

Do you ever wish you could turn back time? Me, too! Well, you're going to enjoy Perfectly Reasonable! The events in Margo's story, Book 2 in the Perfectly Series, actually occur a few years before Book 1 Perfectly Honest. Mikaela makes an appearance because Margo and Mikaela have been best friends for years, and you'll hear more about Chloe, Margo's assistant. This story is all about finding your passion – not easy to do because, of course, it's always in the last place you look!

Laugh every day. Love every minute.

Linda

Chapter 1

Margo MacMillan wished she could take the job. *Look at that view.*

Beyond the picture window and down eighteen floors, waves lapped against the Lake Ontario shore despite frigid January temperatures. Above, it was all blue skies and sunshine. Very Zen.

This side of the window, it was blue eyes and sun-streaked hair. Trace, the pheromone-radiating, sweet-boy-next-door of her current client, was very . . . unZen.

"It has to be done by Tuesday," he insisted.

Fat chance of that happening, considering it was already Friday afternoon. Too bad. He really was . . . breathtaking. "No can do. I have another client lined up for next week."

"Bump them."

Her eyebrows winged up. "I can't do that. They're waiting for me, and I promised to start Monday."

"Trades do it all the time."

She frowned at him. "Not me. If I say I'm going to start a job on Monday, I start on Monday. You'll have to find another painter." Her curls bounced as she turned to go.

"Wait." He touched her arm, and Margo felt a zing of electricity shimmer through her. "You could do it this weekend."

"I don't work weekends."

"I'll pay double."

Margo looked him in the eyes. Eyes that were icy pale blue, almost silver, and too intense to focus on, except they were set in a chiseled face with a square jaw and the most disarming smile.

Her fees were already pretty high. What could possibly be so urgent that he'd pay twice what it was worth?

She glanced around the room. Big open space and pristine beige walls. Sleek leather furniture. Glass, metal, and a zebra-skin rug. And staged for a cover shoot.

What was the deal? Was he desperate to erase the memory of a girlfriend? It was more than possible with the combination of those low-slung jeans, gray T-shirt showing off broad shoulders and flat abs, and that close-cropped blond hair. He towered over her, and she was taller than average. Yeah, it was definitely possible. Or maybe a new ladylove he had to please? She raked her gaze over him. Nah. He wouldn't need a new paint color for that.

She sighed and thought of the student loan she had yet to pay off. If she prepped the walls that evening, she could probably get the painting done by Monday. "All right. But I'd have to start tonight and come back early Saturday and Sunday."

His shoulders relaxed. "Not a problem. I can be here."

"Have you chosen the paint color?"

"No, but it has to be blue."

"Blue?"

"Yes. Pale blue, gray-blue, dark blue, I don't care. Just as long as it's blue."

She shrugged. "Okay then. I'll bring over some paint chips later and you can choose. You'll have to make a decision tonight, so I can stop on my way tomorrow to pick it up."

"I can do that. And I'll invite some of my buddies over to move the furniture."

"That would be great. Just push everything to the center of the room. I can cover it with plastic."

Trace nodded. "Thank you for this. I really appreciate it. I've heard you're the best."

She smiled. Charm and good looks. He'll go far. "You're welcome. I'll finish the job next door and come back at about seven."

"Works for me. See you then."

Margo let herself into the condo next door, calculating how much time she'd need to finish, clean up, and grab a bite to eat. The rich aroma of a spicy stew almost masked the paint fumes.

"How'd it go?"

Margo looked up. "It went well, Mrs. Crombie. I got the job." She gave a crooked smile. Lost her weekend, but cash was cash. "Thanks for the recommendation."

"Oh. I'm going tell all my friends about you, no doubt about that. I love what you've done here. But actually it was Trace who recommended you to me." Green eyes twinkled in a round face surrounded by waves of white hair. Mrs. Crombie wore an apron over her practical tweed skirt and stood in the doorway of the kitchen, holding a wooden spoon.

"Really?" That was the first time she'd met him. How did he know her?

"Yes, dear. I decided I wanted a change. I was a bit worried about having a stranger in my home, and my friend, Emma, had a painter who was absolutely dreadful. Left a mess everywhere. Didn't show up half the time. Charged her more than they agreed. It was a nightmare. One day I mentioned it to Trace. He's such a sweet boy. I tell you, if I was fifty years younger . . ." She wiggled her eyebrows and laughed. "Anyhow, he gave me your name. Said you were excellent. A bit pricey . . ."

Margo winced.

"But excellent. And I'm very happy I called you. It was worth every penny." Mrs. Crombie smiled broadly.

Margo smiled back. "Thank you very much. I've enjoyed working here the past couple of weeks. And I'm glad you're pleased with the result."

"Oh, yes. It's absolutely lovely. I'm sorry it's done. I'm going to miss your company."

"Me, too. I'm going to have a hard time going back to paper-bag lunches. You spoiled me."

Mrs. Crombie threw her head back and laughed. "That's my specialty. After so many years of cooking for six, it's hard to scale back for one. Trace is always happy to take a share. He comes over to do the odd job for me, and I send him home with the leftovers. He's a sweetie."

Margo nodded. "I'm glad he's looking out for you." Made her feel better about giving up her weekend. "I promised I'd start his place tonight."

"Well, I have a nice stew simmering. By the time you get all cleaned up, it will be ready. We can have one last meal together. And I'm going to write down the number of the soup kitchen you mentioned. What did you call it?"

"Breaking Bread."

"Yes. I'd like to get out more, and cooking for others would be a pleasure."

"Definitely. They'd love your help." She'd become attached to Mrs. Crombie. The elderly woman was lonely and had spunk to spare. "And I can vouch for your delicious cooking."

Mrs. Crombie beamed. She waved the spoon in her hand. "Oh, get away with you." She smiled and winked. "I have time to make some apple spice muffins. You could share them with Trace."

Margo smiled. Matchmaking? She couldn't say she minded and hey, bonus, homemade baked goods. "Sounds wonderful."

Chapter 2

Margo stood in the hallway with two huge canvas tote bags over her shoulder and a Tupperware container in her hand. She checked her watch, seven o'clock on the dot, and knocked on the door.

A guy with short brown hair and a boyish face opened the door.

Margo blinked. "Daniel?"

A wide grin split his face. "Hey, Margo. Long time, no see. How are you?" He reached to give her a quick hug. "Let me help you with that stuff." He took one of the tote bags off her shoulder and waved her inside with the hand holding a beer. "You must be the hot painter Trace is expecting," he said with a laugh.

She flicked a glance at Trace who was standing with a group of guys across the room. "I guess I am," she said with a grin. "I can't believe you're here. How do you know Trace?"

"Friend of a friend. We're heading out to the game tonight, but Trace needed some manpower to shift around some furniture, so we stopped by here first. We're just having a beer. You want one?"

"Thanks Daniel, but I'd better not. I have some work to do."

"You sure? Painting and beer sound like they go together." He set the tote down near a window.

She laughed. "Maybe if you're painting an abstract." She shrugged the other tote off her shoulder and Daniel reached over, lifted it, and placed it beside the one on the floor.

"Those are heavy. What have you got in there?"

"All the stuff I need to do a good job," she said.

"I'm going to stop complaining about carrying around medical equipment."

"You just need stronger muscles like me." She flexed her bicep.

He nodded and laughed. "And twenty-five hour days so I can get to the gym."

"How's the residency going? Are you enjoying emergency medicine?"

"Loving it. I haven't seen much of the Emergency Department yet. We're rotating through surgery. I'm in the middle of gen surg right now."

"Wow. Long days I imagine. It's hard to believe you're already halfway through your first year. It goes by fast."

"One day blurs into the next." He took a sip of his beer, hazel eyes watching her closely. "When are you coming back?"

Before she had a chance to answer, Trace came up and gave Daniel a pat on the shoulder. "You two look like you know each other," he said, looking from Daniel to Margo.

Daniel raised his beer to Margo. "Same med school class. Margo here graduated with the gold medal around her neck."

Trace's eyebrows went up.

"Daniel got the silver and was a sore second place finisher."

"It should've been a tie. A difference of half a percent. Literally two multiple choice questions separating us."

"Actually, it's probably closer to five," Trace said, looking at them.

Margo shook her head. "Yeah. Yeah. Heard it all before. That's what you get for choosing to study with Cynthia Peters instead of me." She laughed and brushed imaginary lint off her shoulder.

"You're a doctor?" Trace asked, staring at Margo.

Margo looked at him. "Technically, yes. I have a medical degree." She held out the Tupperware container. "Mrs. Crombie sent these over. Apple spice muffins. She said we should share."

Trace glanced from her to the container and back again.

"Oh, and I have the paint samples here so you can pick a color." She reached down into one of the totes and pulled out a paint fan. "I put stickies on the ones I thought would work."

Trace barely glanced at the colors. "Yeah, one of those would be great." He tilted his head. "Aren't you too young to be a doctor?"

"I hear that a lot. Or at least, I used to," she said with a wry smile. "But no, I'm not. I did two years of undergrad and three years of medicine. No summers off so it was a little faster."

"And more intense," Daniel added. He took another sip of beer.

"But worth it to finish in three years instead of four, right?" Margo asked.

Daniel shrugged. "Maybe. I was just happy to get into any medical school."

Trace nodded. "Do you know the odds of getting into medical school are roughly one in three hundred, depending on the number of applicants? There's more chance of living to a hundred."

As he spoke, one of his friends sauntered over. He bumped Trace's shoulder. "At least when you finally get in, you can have a nice long career," the friend said, clinking his beer bottle with Trace's. "You don't want to rush these things. Better to take your time. Finish your master's degree and think it through."

Trace snorted. "You're just worried about losing your math tutor."

"That's true." He grinned. "Cheers," he said to Margo, raising his beer.

"Hey, we should get going," one of the other guys shouted from across the room. "The game starts in forty minutes."

Trace turned to Margo. "Is the furniture okay where it is?"

The sofa, end tables, and a large cabinet were pushed to the center of the room.

"Yeah, that's perfect. About the color, did you want to choose?"

"Any of your stickies are fine," he said, looking around and patting his pockets. "Hey, Bren, do you have the tickets?"

"I do. Go Cascades! Woohoo!"

Margo looked over and smiled. Someone had enough to drink.

"What time tomorrow morning?" Trace asked Margo.

"Eight."

"Ouch," his buddy said.

Trace shrugged into a jacket and nodded. "See you then."

"Bye, Margo. Keep in touch," Daniel added, giving her a hug.

"Will do. Don't work too hard."

Daniel smirked. "Tweet that to the dean."

She laughed as the group grabbed their jackets and waved good-bye.

Chapter 3

At seven-thirty the next morning, Margo pulled into the parking lot of Paint and Putty, her favorite store in all of Rivermede. She parked her little red Mini-Cooper beside a red BMW and gave a wide berth to the yellow Pontiac. Red car people were the best. Most conscientious drivers, cautiously opened their doors to avoid dinging the car next to them, and followed a regular vacuuming schedule. The complete opposite of yellow car people. Honestly, they should have a separate area of the parking lot.

She opened her car door a crack and slipped out, with plenty of space between her and the BMW. She carried a fan of paint colors in one hand and a coffee in the other as she walked to the contractor's entrance. She shivered and wished she'd taken the time to zip up her coat.

It hadn't taken long to prep the walls the night before, so she spent some time choosing the color. It still surprised her when people left the choice of color to her. Granted it wasn't easy, and she wasn't sure what was worse, too much choice or too little.

After years of working with paint, she knew people saw colors differently. The sun exposure, the furniture, the art on the walls, even the flooring could change how a hue looked in a room.

But more than that, color made her *feel* something. The calm of sea-green, or the energy of orange in a bright room, how could you leave that to someone else? Just slap up any old color? She couldn't imagine. Boy, if she had to look at it and live in it, she'd definitely want to pick it. But to each his own. And since she rarely had to scrap a color and start again, she was either good at picking paint color, or clients.

She had chosen a blue-gray for Trace. It felt strong and looked masculine. It wasn't too fussy or pale for a living room, and with the west sun exposure, the bit of gray would mask any yellow undertones in the blue. She hoped he liked it because she was about to spend a whack of money getting it mixed.

The gray-haired man behind the counter, wearing paint-spattered overalls, greeted her with a smile. "Hey, Doc."

Jerry Fortnight had cheered her on as she'd painted her way through undergrad and medical school. How many times had she sat studying while she waited for paint to be mixed? He probably didn't know how much his unwavering confidence meant to her as she sweated through exams. Nor realized how much his matter-of-fact acceptance of her choosing painting over medicine put him in her heart forever. Margo gave an indulgent smile and handed him the coffee. "For you, my love."

His face lit with pleasure. "Why thank you, sweetheart. Have I got the days mixed up? Isn't today Saturday?"

She laughed. "I know. So unlike me. But I thought I'd chip away at the student loans."

He took a sip of the coffee. "Oh, that's good." He gave her a pointed look. "You should take them up on their offer. Then you could sleep in."

Margo snorted. "You think? I expect a fancy art gallery like Calhoun International would have pretty high expectations. Need a certain number of pieces by a certain date."

"Well, I suppose I wouldn't know. Don't know how to paint those fancy paintings you do. I just sell the paint."

She smiled. "Today I'm painting blank walls. I need three gallons of this blue."

"Coming right up," he said, and took the paint chip.

As he mixed the paint, Margo thought about the offer. She had been painting for as long as she could remember. Probably before she held a crayon. She had once dreamed of having her paintings displayed in a fine gallery, but it wasn't until she was busy with medicine that it had finally happened. The offer was a good one, and she was tempted to take it. She had sold a painting privately and had made half a year's worth of tuition, and now the local, internationally acclaimed, gallery was interested in a show solely of her work. The terms were flexible, and they offered to pay her up front for any paintings she wanted to show. She was busy with commercial and residential painting, still had to figure out what she wanted to do about medicine, and wondered if she wanted the stress of creating under a deadline. Too much choice.

Jerry heaved three cans onto the counter. "There you go. I can help you with them to your car." He shrugged on a jacket and grabbed two of the cans.

They stepped outside into the cold crisp air. "Make sure you get out and enjoy the sunshine. Come Monday, we're expecting snow." His breath puffed out in a frosty cloud.

"I'll be enjoying the sunshine from the warmth indoors today. Thanks, Jerry," she said as he placed the cans in the back.

"Thanks for the coffee." He tipped his ball cap. "We'll see you soon."

Margo hopped in the car, and with a wave, pulled out of the parking lot.

She carried two cans of paint to Trace's condo, leaving the third for another trip. At eight-ten, she knocked on the door.

The door opened and a sleepy-eyed Trace stepped back to invite her in. What was it about morning scruff that had her ovaries hopping? Of course, the bare chest and low-slung gray track pants didn't hurt either.

"Would you like a coffee?" he asked, rubbing a hand down his face.

"No, thanks. I've had mine." She admired the rear view as he disappeared into the kitchen.

She set the paint cans down on the floor and looked at the paint chip sample she had hung on the wall. Looked just as good in the morning light, thankfully.

She covered the floor with drop cloths as the smell of freshly brewed coffee filled the air.

Trace returned to the living room and sat down on a barstool. He sipped his coffee, watching her. "You're pretty chirpy considering the hour."

"I probably had an earlier night than you," she said with a smile. She looked at the empties on the counter. "And no hangover this morning. How was the game?"

"Great. Cascades won."

She nodded. She had watched highlights of the hockey game while she ate breakfast. "Did you have good seats?"

He nodded. "My dad's box," he said absently.

She hid her surprise. Big money there. Box seats were hard to come by. She realized Mrs. Crombie hadn't mentioned his family name, and she hadn't asked.

"So, you're a doctor," he said slowly.

Jeez, back to that. "Yup."

"How come a doctor is painting my living room?"

"Because you're paying twice the usual fee," she said with a cheeky grin.

"Shouldn't you be . . . doctoring?"

Her smile slipped. He sounded like her mother. All that time, all that money, blah, blah, blah. "I could be, but at the moment, I'm painting." She pointed to the paint sample hanging on the wall. "That's the color I chose."

He looked over. "I like it. Hopefully it will work."

"I think it'll work. Blue's a neutral color. Looks good in this lighting, and it'll be a great backdrop for your metal furniture."

"Hmm-mmm. I'm hoping it'll be lucky."

"Lucky?"

"Feng shui. Water and metal elements, á la blue paint and metal furniture in the west and southwest rooms, are supposed to bring divine luck this year. Good–bye beige and wooden antiques."

She smiled at him. He wants to get lucky? Look at those abs. Really, any color would do. "Sounds like you've researched this."

He took a sip of coffee and set the cup down. "I have. I'm applying to medicine. Again. I'm giving it one last chance, and this time I'm doing it properly."

"Medicine."

"Yes."

"And you think feng shui will help?" She reached for a small tool in the outer pocket of the tote bag and used it to pry open the lid from the first can of paint.

"Couldn't hurt. And I want to cover all the bases. If I can get a little divine luck on my side, I'm all for it."

She stirred the paint. Hopefully he had more than feng shui up his sleeve. "I'll get this done and get you started. I'm happy to help." Especially if it meant her bills would get paid.

"Are you? You could be handy."

"Oh, I'm definitely handy," she said with a smile.

Chapter 4

Margo dipped a new brush in the paint can and stepped up on a stool to reach the top of the wall. And felt a little thrill. The first stroke of paint on the wall did that to her. A blank canvas, even a plain wall, made her think of all the possibilities. New color, new outlook, new attitude, and maybe a bit of divine luck, she thought with a smile.

She ran the brush along the edge of the ceiling in a smooth even stroke, aware of Trace's eyes as he followed her movement.

"What would you say is the secret to getting into medical school?" he asked.

She sighed. Didn't he have somewhere he had to be, something else he had to do? "You know, I don't really know."

"Well, you got in. What made your application stand out?"

She stepped down and dipped her brush in the paint. This color was going to be perfect. She knelt down to the baseboard and angled her brush to edge the bottom of the wall. "I honestly don't know. I was surprised to get in."

He snorted. "Come on. Admitted after only two years? That's something." He stood up with his coffee and came closer to watch her work. "My marks are good and my MCAT scores solid. Statistically, I had a better than average chance of getting admitted, but I didn't get a single interview."

Margo glanced over at him as she finished creating the border for an eight-foot swatch of wall. He really was adorable. Tousled hair, pale blue eyes the color of the sky on a sunny day, and the determination of a little kid after a coveted toy. He was close enough that she could smell the musky scent of his skin. His chest was another form of art. She fleetingly wondered if he'd let her paint him. Nude.

"Really, when I calculated the odds, I should have done much better."

Margo set down the brush. "It's more than marks," she said, distracted. Did the paint need to be stirred? She poured the paint into a tray, content to see a homogenous color. She picked up the roller, dipped it in the paint, and drew it across the uneven ridges in the tray to remove the excess paint.

"What do you mean?"

She stepped over to the wall. "Marks are the cut-off, but it's not the heart and soul of it," she said reluctantly. She moved the roller in a V pattern drawing the paint down to the edging at the baseboard before slowly rolling it back up to the ceiling. Uneven color of the first coat filled the wall. "You have to add your own mojo."

"How?"

She sighed and felt a pang of guilt. Helping him get into medicine wasn't really her forte. Now if he wanted to explore why he was much better off choosing another career path, *that* she could help him with. "Why do you want to be a doctor?"

"The money's pretty good."

She laughed and glanced over at him. Uh-oh. He was serious. "No."

"No?"

"Wrong answer. Try again."

His brow furrowed, and he walked over and sat down on the barstool. His bare feet found the lower rung. "I want to help people?"

"Not too sure about wanting to help people?" she asked with a chuckle. She picked up the paintbrush to create the border for another block.

"I know doctors help people, but statistically it's not that impressive. Eighty-five percent of patient visits are for chronic complaints, and less than five percent are actually ever cured."

"But people live longer," she pointed out.

"Sure, with regular frequent doctor visits." He rubbed his fingertips together. "And more money."

Margo rolled her eyes. "What about vaccines and antibiotics? You can't say they haven't made a difference."

"That's true, but ninety-eight percent of infections are viral. A healthy lifestyle and frequent hand washing are really all you need." He raised his hands. "Doctors could be considered superfluous."

Margo held the paintbrush over the paint can and smiled. They had more in common than she thought. "If you feel that way, why are you applying to medical school?"

Trace was silent for a moment. "Because the money's pretty good?" he said, tongue-in-cheek.

Margo laughed and shook her head. "I suppose it is, but an answer like that won't get you in." She tapped the excess paint off the brush and continued to edge near the ceiling. "Why medicine? Why not do something with your undergrad degree?"

"You can only do so much with a math degree."

"You're a mathlete?" she asked with a grin.

Now it was his turn to roll his eyes. "Yup. Honors math with a minor in biochemistry. I'm just finishing up my master's degree."

"The pharmaceutical companies would love you." She stepped down off the stool.

He nodded. "I've had a couple of job offers. But, I don't know. I'd like to try medicine. Maybe a doctor only makes a difference fifteen percent of the time, but it's an important fifteen percent."

"It's not all it's cracked up to be," she said quietly. She bent down and focused on painting the wall above the baseboard. She angled the brush and with a steady hand swept it along in a straight line.

He was silent, but she refused to look at him. She already regretted saying anything.

He sighed. "Maybe. But I have to try."

"Why?"

"For my grandfather."

The sadness in his voice had her looking over at him. He stared out the window with a furrow between his brows.

"Is he pressuring you to be a doctor?" she asked.

Trace set his coffee cup down and got up restlessly. "No." He ran his hand over his face. "He died." A look of utter sadness filled his eyes.

"I'm sorry."

Trace swallowed. "Thanks." He paced around the room, and Margo dipped the brush and knelt back to the wall.

"He was in the hospital last summer for a hip replacement. He was pretty anxious going in, even ambivalent about the whole thing. But a doctor reassured him it was the best thing to do. Told him it was routine and that he'd be able to travel and dance at my wedding," he said with a short laugh. "That isn't going to happen anytime soon, so he was reassured that he'd be around for a very long time."

Margo's heart started pounding as she listened.

"But during the surgery, he had a massive heart attack. He didn't make it." Trace turned his back to her and rubbed his eyes.

Margo's hand trembled and paint smeared on the baseboard that she was trying to avoid. She looked over at Trace. "I'm so very sorry," she whispered, as tears gathered behind her eyes. "What's your grandfather's name?" She didn't really need to ask. It was burned in her memory.

"Ernie Pearce."

Her heart squeezed as guilt flooded her. A familiar nausea rolled in her stomach.

Trace cleared his throat. "He always said to me, 'Boy, you've got a head on your shoulders,'" he mimicked in a gravelly voice. "'Be the one ordering the tests and interpreting the results. Don't stop at the mechanics.'" He shrugged. "I toyed with doing medicine and applied last year, but this time I'm going to do some research and do it right. So any help you can give me . . ."

Margo's mouth went dry. Hadn't she distanced herself enough? Hadn't she paid her dues on this one? She couldn't go through it again. She couldn't do it. She didn't want to get involved. She blew out a breath in frustration. Why couldn't she just paint in peace?

She closed her eyes and sighed. Life was never that easy.

Maybe this was karma. In the grand scheme of things, maybe it would even the scales if she shared what little she knew and helped him with his application. It hadn't been that long since she'd written the essays and done the same research.

She looked at the baseboard and the mess she'd made. She'd be repainting that for him, too.

She stood up and turned to look at him. "I could help you with your application if you want."

"Really? You'd do that?" His eyes lit up.

She nodded. "I can't say I'm an expert by any stretch of the imagination, but I can tell you what worked for me. The application is due in a month?"

"Yes." He strode over, hugged her, and lifted her off her feet in a twirl. "Thank you. Thank you. Thank you." He looked into her eyes as he lowered her back to her feet.

Margo's breasts tingled at the contact against his hard chest, and her breath caught at the interest that flared in his eyes. He was going to kiss her. And she wanted to feel his lips on hers. She wanted to taste him. But a wave of guilt had her taking a step back.

"See, this new paint color is working already," he said with delight.

Chapter 5

"So, where do we start?" Trace asked, rubbing his hands together.

Margo picked up the roller brush. She couldn't paint a straight edge freehand with her hands shaking.

First off, he needed to put a shirt on. The combination of smooth skin, fit muscles, tussled blond hair, and sleepy eyes was potent. Between lust and guilt, she could hardly concentrate.

She dipped the roller and worked at covering the next section of wall. "You're going to be asked why you want to be a doctor. I know it's hard for you, but you have to try to put into words how what happened to your grandfather influenced you. Personal experience is a powerful motivator, but it has to be more than he encouraged you." She cleared her throat. "We can leave that for now if you don't want to think about it . . ."

Trace groaned. "Questions like that make my head hurt." He set his coffee down. "I need food," he said and wandered off to the kitchen.

Margo closed her eyes and put her hand to her stomach to quell the nausea. Would it ever get easier? Would she ever be able to let it go? The scene she tried so hard to forget came rushing back.

Margo walked into the orthopedic clinic and strode over to the desk. "Hi, Cheryl. I'm looking for Ernie Pearce."

"Room five," Cheryl said. "Are you the clinical clerk doing pre-op physicals today?"

"I am," Margo said.

"He's had the blood work, chest x-ray, and ECG done. Just needs the physical exam. He said he had some questions for you, too."

"That's why I'm here," Margo plucked a pen from a holder on the desk.

"Bring that back when you're done." Cheryl gave her a mock stern look. "How come you guys never have a pen on you?"

"Because scrubs don't have pockets," Margo said, pointing to the loose cotton clothing she wore that was the standard uniform for the operating room. "Luckily, stethoscopes fit around our necks. Otherwise we'd be borrowing those, too."

Cheryl laughed and waved her away. "Just bring it back."

Margo grinned and headed down to room five. She knocked on the door and went in.

An older gentleman, dressed in slacks and a plaid shirt, a cane by his side, turned to look at her.

"Hi. I'm Margo MacMillan." She closed the door behind her. "I'm the medical student working with Dr. West. He asked me to come and do a brief history and physical exam, if that's okay with you."

"Yes, of course. It's quite the rigmarole for a new hip."

Margo sat down in front of him. "Well, this is the last of it. The nurse mentioned that everything else is done." She checked the papers she held. "Your surgery is scheduled for next week?"

"Yes. June twenty-second. Hopefully, early in the morning."

"Did Dr. West explain the procedure to you?"

He nodded. "Fred was in here earlier and went over the whole deal. Gave me more information than I wanted to know."

"We like to be thorough." Margo went through the medical questions she needed to ask and learned that he was a widower living on his own. His wife, Rose, had passed away six months ago, and Margo felt the love as he chatted about how she had taken care of him. "You miss her," she said quietly.

"Every day."

"That must be hard. Do you have other family?"

"I have a daughter, Anita. She's been great. She lives in town with her husband and two sons. We're close." He hesitated. "I have a question, but how much of this do you pass on or write down?"

"Everything we talk about is confidential."

Ernie nodded. "Could I ask you something off the record, so-to-speak? Fred's a great doctor. I'm glad to have him. But he's also a golfing buddy of mine, and I couldn't ask him . . ." He shifted restlessly and looked at her with worried eyes. "This is a routine procedure, right? Wham, bam, I'm home again."

"Yes, absolutely. It's Dr. West's specialty. He's very good. You don't need to worry."

He pressed his lips together. "I'm not really worried about the surgery per se. But, there is something else."

Margo sat quietly, as emotion thickened his voice.

He swallowed and continued, "When we were young, Rose and I had a baby. Out of wedlock." He gave a crooked smile. "Times were different then. We wanted to get married, but her family would have nothing to do with it. Rose went away, had the baby, and it was never mentioned again. She knew it was a girl, but they didn't let her see it. Damn near broke her heart." He swallowed again and looked off in the distance. "Damn near broke mine.

"I didn't go away as her family had hoped, and we were married the following year. Best decision I ever made." He adjusted his cane and held it with two hands. "Every year on the baby's birthday, we set aside money in a special account, figuring eventually we'd donate it to a children's charity. We never tried to find the child, never spoke of her. To our families, it was like she never existed, but for us, the heartache never went away.

"After Rose died, I was on the computer." He tilted his head. "Quite the invention, that computer. There's a registry where you can look up all the details of an adoption. Finding the baby became the single most important thing for me to do." Fierce determination spread over his features and his eyes filled.

Margo started to speak, but he stopped her. "No, it's okay. There's a happy ending. I found her. They named her Gwen. She's married and has a son, and they live about an hour away." He wiped his eyes. "I see Rose in her."

Margo handed him a tissue. "It's really lovely that you were able to connect."

"It is. I'm very grateful. I would never have been able to do it ten years ago." Ernie shook his head and sighed. "But I haven't told my daughter, Anita. It's been a secret for so long. I don't want to betray my wife, and yet, I feel Anita should know." He looked at Margo. "I'm also selfish – I want more time with Gwen. I don't want to die just yet."

"Oh no, don't worry about that, Mr. Pearce. This procedure is very common. With a little bit of physio, you'll be up and about in no time."

Ernie closed his eyes briefly and his shoulders relaxed. "Thank you. When Fred went on about all the possible complications, that's the only thing that stuck. The thought of death brings urgency to things I never considered urgent. I could put off the surgery or tell Anita now, but I'd rather wait until she can meet Gwen."

Margo patted Ernie's hand. "It'll be okay, you'll see. You'll have time for that and a lot more besides. You'll be dancing at your grandson's wedding."

Ernie laughed. "That's grand. What a relief. Thank you very much."

Margo listened to his heart and lungs and filled out the paperwork. One week later, she reassured him again before they wheeled him into the operating room. She told him she would see him after the surgery.

He died of a massive heart attack on the table before the medical team could save him. Margo was numb. That wasn't how it was supposed to go.

Ernie didn't see Gwen again.

He didn't say good-bye.

He didn't tell Anita she had a sister.

And Margo had to live with the fact that her reassurance was gravely inappropriate.

Margo straightened and rolled the paint on the wall, letting the rhythm and color soothe her. She completed half of another section before Trace returned with two plates and a plastic container.

He pulled open the lid and inhaled. "Mmmm. Apple muffins. Would you like one?"

Margo shook her head. "Maybe in a few minutes. I'd like to get the first coat on." And the nausea settled.

He bit into one. "Delicious," he murmured. "Okay, where were we? Why do I want to be a doctor? Let's see, not for the money." He broke off a piece of the muffin and popped it in his mouth. "I have my doubts about the whole 'helping people' thing. And not because my grandfather told me I should."

"No," she agreed. "It's a long haul and a way of life. You'd better be passionate about it and not be doing it to please someone else."

"Right." He chewed thoughtfully. "Doctors have a lot of power. Look how a few words made a difference to my grandfather."

She winced. "You can't become a doctor so you can wield power like a . . . big stick."

He smiled and waved his hand in the air. "I was thinking more like a magic wand."

She snorted. "It's the wizard, not the wand. Doctors strive to minimize the power. The whole patient–centered interaction is about giving patients choices and putting informed decision-making in their hands."

"Okay. Okay. Jeez. You'd think I said I wanted to get my hands on drugs."

"Oh my God. Don't even joke about that."

He chuckled. "Those admissions people don't have a sense of humor?"

"None," she said emphatically.

"Okay. How about I want to score with the nurses?"

"I don't think you'd need a medical degree for that," she said wryly. She eyed the sculpted muscles of his broad chest and the bulge of his thighs through the track pants he wore. Between that and the shimmer of laughter in his gorgeous blue eyes, he was pretty much irresistible.

He grinned. "Get a big line of credit?"

"Can't tell you how much fun debt is." She set the roller down and picked up the brush.

"I want to be able to say 'Get me that bedpan STAT,' and people will rush to do it."

She laughed. "They'll be hitting you over the head with it."

"How about . . . it's all I ever wanted. Ever since infancy, I've dreamed of becoming a doctor. In fact, my first word was 'stethoscope.'"

"And right on the heels of that was 'big fat liar.'"

He laughed and took a sip of coffee. "All kidding aside, the one thing that does interest me is medical research. The number of studies with flawed statistical analysis is astounding. And appalling, actually. I think I could make a difference there." He finished the last of the muffin and wiped his hands on his pants. "Plus, I find the human body fascinating."

Margo gave him a sharp look to see if he was joking. She flushed at the hunger in his eyes. He was going to have to tone that down, she thought with a shiver. "That's good," she said. "Those answers are perfectly reasonable. And you almost sounded sincere."

"Thank you." He looked pleased. "I was. Although I find some bodies more fascinating than others . . ."

"So close," she murmured, shaking her head, "and yet, so far."

His eyes twinkled. "What's next?"

Chapter 6

Margo moved over to the archway at the door of the condo. She carefully filled in the area around the light switch where the roller couldn't reach and angled the brush to paint around the door. "What other skills do you have?"

Silence.

She glanced over at him. "What else are you good at?"

"Weeeelll," he said with a wide grin.

Margo turned back to her painting. A ripple of awareness ran through her at the picture *that* created in her head. "Uh-uh," she acknowledged, when she found her voice. "We're looking for skills you can write on your resume."

"I know CPR. I've even used it once."

"Wow."

"Yes. Resuscitating a dog."

She raised her eyebrows at him.

"What? It was a tense situation," he said.

"I'm sure it was, but you'll need a little more. What else have you got?"

"Let me get my application." He disappeared down the hall, and when he returned carrying his laptop, he had changed into jeans and a long-sleeved navy sweater. She tried not to stare at his very fine ass. The sweater hugged his broad shoulders and made his eyes look bluer. And what was it about a guy in bare feet that she found so sexy?

He set his laptop on the counter and opened it. "Okay, let's see. Small animal rescue," he read and looked over hopefully.

"That's good. Be better if you were applying to be a veterinarian, but still, it shows compassion. What did you do?"

He rubbed his chin. "I, ah, mostly scooped chipmunks and mice out of our pool."

"Eww."

"I know. They're not very good swimmers."

Margo shook her head. "What else?"

"I worked as a volunteer firefighter."

"That's impressive." She looked over. "For people, right?"

"Technically, yes. Although we lived quite far from the fire station, so by the time I got there, the pumper truck had usually left."

"Did you join them?"

He looked sheepish. "It wasn't usually necessary. But I always helped with the post-call maintenance – cleaning the truck, putting away the hoses – that kind of thing."

"What else?"

"I volunteered at the hospital."

"Excellent. Shows that you've tried to understand what medicine is all about. What did you do there?"

"Mostly worked in the gift shop." He shrugged. "They needed some muscle to organize their stock."

"Any patient interaction at all?"

"Not unless they came in to buy something."

She grimaced.

"Last year, I organized and led a group called the Venn Diagrams at school."

She was afraid to ask.

"They were trying to remove the vending machine from the graduate student lounge, and we successfully petitioned against it. I'm happy to say our access to Coke and Crunchie bars went uninterrupted."

She groaned. "Trace, that's terrible."

"What? Leadership skills," he pointed out.

"For a cause against good health. You're aiming to be a health promoter."

"The grad students were very happy. Whatever happened to 'everything in moderation is okay?'"

"Sure, if there's a balance. Did you fight for anything healthy? Fruit in the lobby? Children's breakfast programs?"

"Seriously? No." He threw his hands in the air. "Coke in the lounge was our one and only cause." He sighed impatiently and closed his laptop with a snap. "That's it. That's all I've got."

She waved the paintbrush at him. "You have some serious volunteering to do in the next four weeks."

"Should I book a trip to a third world country?" he said with a wince.

"Some people do." She grabbed a rag and dabbed at the paint on her hand. "But there are plenty of places here in Rivermede that could use your help."

"I wouldn't even know where to begin. And why exactly am I doing this?"

"Because you need to show that you're a people person. That you can interact and work with others, for starters. And that you can show compassion and be empathetic."

"Doesn't sound like me."

She smiled. "You can learn. You've got four weeks. Luckily you're bright and . . ." She raised an eyebrow at him. ". . . motivated?"

"Yeah. Yeah. Caring and compassionate. That's what I aspire to be," he said dryly. "So what do I do?"

"Pick something you enjoy. If you're going to volunteer, you should be enthusiastic about it."

"Like what? What did you do?"

"A few things. I donated a couple of my paintings to a charity, and they auctioned them off to raise money."

"How much did they go for?"

She gave him an impatient glance and debated whether to tell him. "Five thousand," she said reluctantly.

His eyes widened. "Dollars?"

She fluttered her eyes at him modestly. "People are more generous when the money is going to a charity."

"Wow." He looked at her with respect in his eyes. "I don't paint, so that's not an option."

"Maybe not. But you're good at math."

He nodded. "I used to study in the math hall, but it got annoying because the first and second-year students always came to me for help."

"Tutoring."

He shrugged. "Yeah, I guess so."

"*That* should be on your resume."

"Really? It probably added up to over ten hours a week. I had to put the brakes on it, so I could get my work done."

"Yes, definitely. Teaching is a huge part of medicine. Plus everyone learns differently, and you probably had to tailor how you taught to the student. Communication Skills 101. That's good. Time management is another important skill. So don't focus on why you stopped, but think about how you made it work. Like having scheduled time to tutor and set time to study. Plus bonus, people skills."

"Hat trick," he said with a grin.

"You might want to work on the empathy part, though. I volunteer at Breaking Bread. It's a soup kitchen that offers hot dinners three hundred and sixty-five days a year. They're always looking for help," she hinted.

He grimaced. "Do they like KD and tube steaks?"

She laughed. "We do a little better than Kraft Dinner and hot dogs. But don't worry, you won't have to cook. There's a whole team working together and plenty of other jobs."

"Okay, sounds reasonable. If you think I could help, I'm in."

She hid a smile. Progress? Him offering to help without considering what he could get out of it. That was encouraging.

"I wonder if I should start by eating there. Really get into the empathy thing," he added.

And maybe not.

Chapter 7

Two walls down and two to go. Plus, the wall of windows would be quick with only a strip across the top needing paint. She had made good time and could afford a break for lunch. Margo set her brush down and arched her back, stretching stiff muscles. "I'd love one of those muffins now."

Trace indicated for her to sit and pushed the container of muffins closer. "Help yourself."

She grabbed her lunch and sat down on the bar stool beside him. "I brought a salad if you'd like to share." She reached for a muffin and peeled the paper wrapper off.

"Thanks. Mrs. Crombie sent over some pumpkin soup the other day. Would you like some with your salad?"

"Sounds delicious."

Trace went into the kitchen and as she ate the muffin, she watched him pour the soup into a pot and heat it up. He ladled the steaming soup into two bowls, and her mouth watered. Could have been the warm scent of pumpkin and nutmeg filling the air, but his easy grace and relaxed movements did it, too. He may not cook, but he was smokin' hot in the kitchen. He set the bowls down on the island.

She wrapped her hands around the warm bowl, leaned over it, closed her eyes, and sniffed deeply. "Mmmm . . . thank you."

Trace looked at her with hungry eyes, and she faltered a moment, startled at the thought that he might be reading her mind. "My pleasure," he said. "Here's a spoon." He held it out and when she reached for it, he leaned closer. "It's good for spooning . . ."

She raised startled eyes to his.

". . . soup," he whispered. He chuckled as he walked around the island to join her, and Margo tried not to squirm in her seat.

Feigning nonchalance, she put a portion of her salad on a plate for Trace. Time to change the subject. "I invited Mrs. Crombie to help out at Breaking Bread, too. She's such a great cook."

Trace nodded. "She'd enjoy that. She misses cooking for a crowd, although I'm always happy to take any leftovers."

"She kept me well fed for the two weeks I worked on her condo." Margo pulled her salad closer and picked up her fork. "She said you gave her my name. I was curious about that because we'd never met." She would have remembered.

"From my dad. You come highly recommended. He won't let anyone else paint for him."

Margo blinked. His dad was a client? "Your last name is Pearce?"

"No, that's my maternal grandfather. My last name is Bennett. My dad is Brett Bennett."

Margo's hand stilled. "Bennett Homes." The biggest developer in Rivermede.

Trace dug into the salad. "This is delicious. Yup. That's him. As a matter of fact, he owns this building. I was only allowed to change the paint color if you did the job."

She smiled weakly and her heart sank. She wondered if Brett Bennett would feel the same way if he knew her connection with his father-in-law. "That's a compliment."

"Something he doesn't give lightly. He mentioned you'll be busy this summer with his new development."

That was the plan. Bennett Homes was going to be her major source of income from early spring all the way into the fall. It had been thrilling to win the contract, and it meant steady work for her and Chloe, her assistant.

She poked at her salad. "Thanks for the recommendation to Mrs. Crombie. I appreciate it." She pushed her salad away.

"Not gonna eat that?" Trace asked.

She shook her head and handed it to him. He switched his empty plate for hers and polished it off. Then he started on the soup with the same gusto.

"How does your father feel about you applying to medicine?" she said, stirring her soup slowly.

"He's totally on board. Thinks it's a great idea."

More incentive for her to help him. Maybe if Trace got into medicine, it would balance the wrong she'd done to his family. She took a few spoonfuls of soup, but her appetite was gone. "I should get back to work," she said, standing.

He scraped the side of his bowl to get the last spoonful. "I have to get going, too. I'm playing squash this afternoon." He gathered his plate and bowl. "With your old boyfriend," he said, with a small smile.

Margo's head jerked in surprise as she gathered her dishes. Medical school and a part-time job painting didn't leave much time for boyfriends. But the mildly jealous tone was lovely. "Which one?" she drawled.

Trace laughed. "Daniel."

Margo smiled with pleasure. She'd never dated Daniel, but would have. She had played a game or two of squash with him though. "Oh, good luck. He's good competition."

She took a step forward, her bowl in one hand and the plate in the other, expecting to follow Trace into the kitchen. But he turned and stood still at her comment. Her breasts brushed against his chest and his mesmerizing blue eyes looked into hers. She could smell the fresh scent of his skin, and her heart skipped a beat.

"Is he?" he asked.

"Wh–What?" she stammered.

"Competition?"

A tingle shimmered from her breasts to her belly. Good thing their hands were full. Neither of them needed this complication. "He's very good at . . ." She swallowed. ". . . squash."

Trace's eyes smoldered. "You and I will have to play sometime so you'll have something to compare."

She felt her nipples harden. Her brain was bathed in hormone heaven and refused to think. "Okay." Okay? She winced inside. This gorgeous specimen with the frosty eyes invites her to play and all she could muster was okay?

"Great." Trace smiled broadly. "It's a date."

He turned and headed to the kitchen. Margo blew out a breath and wondered what she'd just agreed to. Trace set his dishes on the kitchen counter and disappeared down the hallway. Margo carried hers into the kitchen, rinsed them, and loaded the dishwasher.

She wandered back to the living room and Trace came out carrying a squash racket. She flipped the lid off a new paint can and stirred it, avoiding his eyes.

Trace came over and squatted down beside her. "Thanks for all your help. Will you still be here when I get back?"

Margo checked her watch. "I'll probably be gone for today, but I'd like to come back tomorrow morning at about ten and finish up."

Trace smiled. "No problem. See you then." He leaned over and brushed her hair behind her ear. Before she could react, he pulled back. He stood and shrugged on a jacket. Whistling a tune, he let himself out of the condo.

Margo sat back on her heels. What had she gotten herself into?

Chapter 8

Later that night, cozy in her own apartment, Margo eased into the bathtub and lowered herself into the steaming water. Bubbles rose to cover her shoulders, and the soft scent of lavender surrounded her. The warmth seeped into her bones, and her mind slowed. As she settled back, she lifted her hand and blew the bubbles into the air. She let the water flow between her fingers.

Guilt tried to creep into the edges of her mind, but she let it swirl and flow away. There had been a day when it would have stayed and circled around endlessly. But she had given herself permission to make her bath a worry-free zone. Only happy thoughts, only positive images were allowed.

She tried to conjure up the image of her happiest moment. When had she been truly, deeply happy? Dance around the room and celebrate happy? She sighed. It had been a while. Probably three and a half years ago, she thought reluctantly.

Margo and Mikaela sat cross-legged facing each other on Margo's bed, still in pajamas, their laptops closed on their laps.

"Are you ready to do this?" Mikaela asked with a lift of her eyebrow.

"No." Margo wrung her hands. Her curly hair, never tame at the best of times, was pulled back in a loose pile on her head. She looked at Mikaela. Her best friend was cool as a cucumber and without the dark circles she was pretty sure she sported. "It would mean big change," she pointed out.

Mikaela sighed. "I know. But good change. It's what we want."

Margo nodded. She wanted it desperately. That's why it was so stressful. "Okay. Let's open them together. And no holds barred. If one of us gets in, we celebrate, even if the other doesn't." They had talked about that. They wanted to be there for each other, good news or bad. They had to keep in mind that they'd only just finished second year and getting into medical school was a long shot.

Mikaela tucked her long brown hair behind her ear. "On the count of three. One, two, three."

They opened their laptops and waited for their email to download. All the offers were supposed to be sent out at 8 a.m.

Margo held her breath as the icon whirred and an email downloaded.

Cantech University Congratulations! You have been accepted...

She gasped and covered her mouth with her hands, her heart leaping.

Mikaela sat still, watching her screen intently. Then she raised shining eyes to Margo. "I got in," she said.

"Me too," Margo breathed.

They screamed, jumped up, and hugged. They bounced around the room holding onto each other.

"I can't believe it," Margo said, shaking her head.

"I'm so happy, so happy." Mikaela danced around the room.

Margo did a fast jog on the spot and ended with a twirl. "We did it. We actually did it!" She grinned from ear to ear. "This is the best day of my life." Pure joy raced through her, and she pumped her arms and jumped three feet in the air.

Mikaela laughed. "I know. Woohoo!"

"I really didn't think we'd get in." She looked at Mikaela with wide eyes. "I hoped and crossed my fingers and toes."

She plopped down on the edge of the bed. "But I really didn't think it would happen this year."

Mikaela sat down beside her. "I'm glad we'll be together. I'd be scared on my own."

Margo wrapped her arm around Mikaela's shoulders and squeezed. "Big scary change?"

Mikaela nodded. "We'll share a place again?"

"Absolutely." Margo flopped back on the bed. "Oh man. This is amazing. I really wanted this, but I was afraid to hope."

Mikaela smiled at her. "Life is good," she said with a laugh. "I need to call my parents." She stood. "Are you going to call your mom?"

"Eventually," Margo said with a sigh. "I think I'll bask a little longer."

"She'll be proud, you know."

"Yeah, maybe. But I just want to savor this sweet moment a little while longer before she rains on my parade."

Some of the light dimmed from Mikaela's face.

"Don't you worry about my mom. It'll be fine," She waved Mikaela away. "Go. Call your parents and let them in on the excitement. They'll be thrilled."

Mikaela grinned. "They will." She leaned over and squeezed Margo's hand. "I'm so glad we'll be in this together."

"Definitely a celebration tonight. Tomorrow we'll plan."

Mikaela skipped out of the room to call her parents. Margo picked up her phone, and after debating a moment, slowly punched in her mother's number.

She wiggled her toes in the water and swirled the bubbles around. That was probably the happiest moment.

Unfortunately brief, but intense.

The phone call to her mother had been what she had expected. Yes, tuition was going to be expensive. Yes, she would find the money herself. No, she wouldn't expect a handout. Yes, it would be another three years before she graduated.

Stop.

Margo took a deep cleansing breath and focused on the bubbles. Noticed how the light split into a rainbow of color on each surface, how the bubbles stacked into a pyramid when she scooped them lazily together, and how they swirled in the water as she stirred the surface. She inhaled the perfume in a deep breath and blew it out slowly.

Focus. Happy thoughts.

Mikaela made her happy. Mikaela's parents had thrown a huge party. Of course, they loved entertaining and were always looking for a reason to celebrate. All of Palent, Mikaela's father's company, was invited. Fancy duds, fancy food, in a fancy five-star hotel. She was invited too and basked in the overflow of well-wishing and pride. Mikaela's parents were the absolute best. So different from her own.

Well, her mom, anyway. The only memory of her dad was from the photograph on her nightstand, cuddled on his lap when she was three. As hard as she tried, she couldn't bring him to life. Maybe that's why her mom seemed so distant. Maybe losing your husband to heart disease and carrying the weight of raising a young child on your own took its toll.

Margo shivered in the tepid water and pulled the plug. Why did focusing on the positive take so much energy?

She stood, stepped out of the tub, quickly dried off in the cool air, and belted a thick terry robe around her waist. She didn't need to clear the steam from the mirror as she pulled out the clip holding her curls and poked a pik through her hair. Trying to tame the curls after a bath was impossible.

Her bed looked inviting with the flannel sheets and fluffy duvet. She crawled in, pulled the covers to her chin, and leaned back against the pillows.

It was time to change the color on the walls. The olive green was soothing and quiet, and matched her mood a year ago, but she was ready for a little bit of happy. An orange-yellow maybe – the heat of the Mexican sun mixed with a relaxing siesta. Or the purple of Mardi Gras. Not too bright, though. Maybe a subtle mauve, with a little white to make it pop. She could do that.

Or blue. For a bit of divine luck, she thought with a small smile.

Heaven knows she needed it.

She wanted her life to be settled, to go a day without guilt. To be content with the decisions she made and the path she chose.

She opened the drawer of her nightstand and reached for her journal. It was a journal entry kind of day. If she could write it down, maybe she could convince herself to let it go. At least for eight hours of sleep.

She hesitated, then pushed aside the bright orange and yellow flowered one, and lifted out the well-worn book underneath.

She ran her hand over the cover, brushing the nap of the velour. It was a deep magenta. Because pink helps you think, she remembered telling herself. Her heart felt heavy as she stared at the cover. On the first day of medical school, a wizened old clinician had suggested keeping a journal. She had lapped up every suggestion and had bought it that day at the bookstore, not really understanding why it would be so valuable.

She opened the cover. Three years ago her writing had been a lot easier to read.

Aug. 23, 2010 First day

Still floating on cloud nine. Can't believe I'm here. I looked around the classroom today at eighty other smiling faces. They put the stethoscope around my neck and I vowed to listen to the patient. Hard to do with all that singing and celebrating going on in my head!

Aug. 24, 2010

First full day of classes. They don't fool around. 9 to 5 every day. Figured out why all the notes are online — 200 pages of notes just from the lectures today! Hoping my brain is big enough.

Aug. 28, 2010

Went out for a drink with the class. A few strange ones, making note of their names so family members can avoid. Thank goodness for Mikaela (again). Some random guy at the bar found out I was a medical student and showed me his rash. Doesn't he realize I know NOTHING?? Except maybe detailed minutiae of arm anatomy.

Aug. 31, 2010

Went to bank to sort out loan. Healthy bank account from summer and a few jobs lined up on weekends, but tuition is sick. The nonchalant 'of course we can start a whopping big credit line for you,' no questions asked, was a glimpse into the elite world. Wonder if it would work at Tim Hortons??? Free java for a good cause.

Sept. 21, 2010

Studying anatomy of the pelvis. Books, online 3D images, models, lots of resources, but just not getting it. Felt like biggest dummy, until we dissected out the layers in the cadaver lab. Smell of formaldehyde aside, best learning experience ever. Deepest gratitude. Came home and signed my donor card.

Sept. 27, 2010

Aha! moment: maybe fingerprints are unique, but insides are exactly the same! Organs, muscles, arteries, nerves— same place in EVERY body. How cool is that! Even if I'm halfway across the world, can't speak the language, don't have to worry that they won't find my appendix! Makes me want to travel more.

Aug. 8, 2011

Managed to sneak into second year. Decent marks (maybe they mixed up my exam with someone else's???)

Oct. 14, 2011

Fear my brain will explode. Not sure where all the information is going, but hoping the retrieval system will be in place when I actually need all this.

Nov. 9, 2011

Pop quiz scare today. One classmate got up and walked out (if she didn't write it, there'd be no mark). Turns out it was an endocrinology lesson on adrenalin and the flight or fight response. The professor thought it went well.

Dec. 12, 2011

Getting used to examining patients. Whole new ballgame with the male genital exam. Lotta blood flow when the spotlight is focused there. Outward calm, inward panic.

Jan. 10, 2012

Aunt Pauline asking about fever and diarrhea post-Caribbean holiday. Still know NOTHING.

March 8, 2012

How does anyone stay healthy? Soooo many things can go wrong . . .

April 17, 2012

Scary day tomorrow. Clerkship Day 1. Eighty new 'holy cow you're relying on us to actually do something' invade the hospital. Not a good day to be sick.

May 26, 2012

End of resp rotation. NEVER SMOKE. Don't think about smoking. Stay away from smoky bars/restaurants. Don't marry/date/one-night-stand with a smoker. Don't even listen to 'You Light Up My Life.' No lungs = oxygen in a backpack = *shudder*

June 30, 2012

Ruled out doing pediatrics. Poor Olivia. Two years old and yet another transfusion. She screamed the whole time the IV was in. I know she needs it, but heartbreaking just the same. At the delivery of a stillborn – 22 weeks. Baptized the baby for the mom. Diagnosed diabetes in a five-year-old. Needles for life. Hard day.

Sept. 24, 2012

Called to a delivery. Where was the staff??? The cord was around the baby's neck and snapped when I tried to remove it. Baby alive but anemic. Mom has huge tear. Resident (who sauntered in LATE) told me to suture it, but just looked like a huge bloody mess. There are layers?? I didn't see layers. Had visions of creating track into rectum, sewing vaginal walls together. Couldn't do it. Resident not very happy with me. (That's okay, I'm not very happy with me either.)

Oct. 10, 2012

Met Clarisse. I'll be following her through the year. Five foot seven inches and one hundred pounds. Very scary. Super nice teenager, but adamant won't be admitted. Quiet, but seems to want help. Screening tests done for anorexia. Hooked her up with dietician and food bank. First goal – gain some weight.

Dec. 9, 2012

Family medicine not what I thought. Hordes of the weak and dizzy, unsolvable problems. Does no one take ownership of their health??

Dec. 25, 2012

On call

Jan. 11, 2013

Meeting Clarisse weekly. Weight now 104 lb. She's still not out of the woods for risk of cardiac event, but on the right path. I don't really understand how she got to this point. What questions should I be asking?

Feb. 2, 2013

On call 1 in 3. Sleep, work all day and night, stay until noon, sleep, repeat. Haven't read a newspaper, listened to the radio. Way behind in 'Breaking Bad.'

April 3, 2013

Too tired to care.

May 4, 2013

Clarisse's father died of bowel cancer. Clarisse's mom had an affair while her father coped with dying. Parents can really mess up a child.

June 22, 2013

Can't do this. Watched a patient die on the operating table. I told him he would be fine. I told him not to worry. Can't stop the tears. Can't do this anymore. I need to paint.

Margo looked at the tear stains that covered the page and blurred the words.

It had taken until mid-September before she felt like she deserved to live.

By mid-October, she could sleep through the night.

By Christmas, she had built up her painting business again and finished a few therapeutic canvases that sold well. Nothing like angst in a work to seal the emotion. Creativity in a crisis seemed to work very well for her.

And here she was in mid-January. She closed the journal with a sigh and rubbed her hand over the cover. Smooth and soft. She brushed the nap watching it go from shiny to dull.

She set it back in the drawer and pulled out the smaller one covered in bright orange and yellow flowers. A Christmas gift to herself that she hadn't yet used. She cracked open the spine and picked up a pen.

She stared off in the distance and wondered why she bothered.

She felt guilty. Writing it down hadn't helped in the past. Keeping a journal just reminded her how awful she was. What was the point of trying again? She closed the book with a snap and threw it in the drawer. Slamming the drawer shut, she clicked off the light and flounced back against the pillows. Stupid process. Whoever came up with that?

She stared at the ceiling and wished for sleep.

Chapter 9

Margo huffed out a breath and glanced at the clock on the dashboard. Just her luck to get behind a green van. She didn't need the green-van treatment this morning.

Her alarm had startled her out of a deep sleep, mainly because the deep sleep didn't happen until three in the morning. She had burned her tongue on her coffee, her hair was a mess, and her brain still in a fog. She was going to have to make a detour for another coffee. And the brake happy, 'it's-such-a-nice-day-let's-admire-the-scenery' green van wasn't even hitting the speed limit.

Holy cow, could you drive any slower? She stared at the little stick figure drawings of a dad, mom, four children, dog, and two cats on the back windshield of the van. Great. Potentially four more green van people in the wings. Just what the world needed.

She threw her left blinker on and cut around the corner. She accelerated a hundred feet and cut into the Tim Hortons drive-thru. And groaned. There were at least eight cars inching toward the window. She didn't have time for that.

She made a uey, her wheels screeching, pulled out onto the road, and gave a large sigh. What were the chances of Trace having coffee ready?

Margo unbuttoned her coat and knocked on the door of Trace's condo. She shifted the can of paint she carried to the opposite hand and glanced at the time. Ten-fifteen. She hated being late. She knocked again with a little more force.

The door opened with a flourish.

"Hold onto your hat, sweet pea, I'm here." Trace flashed her a brilliant smile and waved her inside.

Margo scowled and walked in. She set the can of paint down and slipped off her coat.

"And good morning to you, too," Trace said with a laugh. "Coffee?"

"Please," said Margo. She toed off her shoes and looked at the different colored socks she wore. They had looked the same in the dim light of her bedroom. Grimacing, she slipped them off and stuffed them in her shoes. Hopefully Trace wouldn't notice.

She brushed a curl impatiently from her face and looked around at the walls.

The color looked good. A quiet settled in, and her body relaxed as she turned in a circle and looked at all the walls. The blue was perfect. There were streaks here and there, definitely needed a second coat, but it looked good.

She smelled fresh brewed coffee and inhaled deeply. Need. Need. Need. Trace walked into the room with a steaming mug. Want.

He wore gray sweatpants and a navy hoodie with the Bennett Homes logo. He handed her the coffee with a smile and didn't say a word.

Margo took a sip and closed her eyes on a groan. "Delicious. Thank you."

"My pleasure."

Margo caught his glance and looked away at the twinkle in his eye.

"Can I help with anything?" he asked.

Margo took a few more sips and felt the buzz of caffeine burn away the fog. "It's not necessary. I'll get the tarps down again and the second coat on. How do you like the color?"

He looked around the room, nodding. "Looks good. I didn't think it would change the room so much."

She raised her eyebrows at him. "In a good way? Or bad?"

"Definitely good. The followers of feng shui know what they're doing."

Margo laughed. "It'll be even better once it's done."

She set her coffee down and pulled out a tarp to cover the floor. Trace grabbed one end and unfolded it until it reached the wall.

Margo set out a paint tray and reached for the tool to open the paint can. "How was your squash game?"

Trace took a seat by the island. "Good. I won." He sipped his coffee. "If you ever want to start a fan club, Dan the Man could be president."

Margo looked over at him, startled. "What?"

"He had only good things to say about you."

"Must have been a short conversation."

"Just the opposite. Said you were dedicated, hard-working, brilliant–"

Margo snorted.

"Compassionate, creative, respected–"

Margo squirmed and frowned. "Holy cow. Didn't you have anything more interesting to talk about?" *How much did Daniel know about her and Ernie Pearce? How much did he say?* Her hand shook as she pried open the lid.

Trace grinned. "Nope. I was all ears."

Margo was silent, frantically thinking about how to change the topic.

"You know what else he said?" Trace teased.

"You talk too much?"

Trace laughed. "Nope. He said he really hopes you go back to medicine."

Margo picked up the stir stick and slowly dipped it in the can. She swirled the paint, careful not to spill any over the edge.

"No comment?" Trace asked quietly.

"No comment." A heaviness settled in her chest.

Trace came over and crouched down beside her. "Hey."

Margo couldn't look at him.

Trace covered her hand with his. "I didn't mean to make you sad," he said in a low voice. "Dan said it was a huge loss when you dropped medicine. He seems to have his shit together, so I took that as a pretty big compliment." He squeezed her hand. "You should, too."

She nodded silently.

"Plus, I was reassured you were qualified to help me."

She looked at him grinning, and smiled reluctantly. "Checking my credentials, eh?"

"Of course." He stood. "Don't want just any hack giving me advice."

She shook her head with a laugh. "Nice that I come so highly recommended. Hope I live up to that."

"Yup. So what's next?"

"Empathy. Making you care."

"How much time you got?" he joked.

She rolled her eyes and poured paint into the tray. "Okay here's the scenario. A twenty-six-year-old single mom brings her three-year-old daughter into the Emergency Department with severe asthma. The child ends up in the intensive care unit intubated and on a respirator. Mom smokes at home. This is the third time the child has been admitted. There's some discussion about whether the child needs to be put in foster care. How would you talk to the mom about this?"

"I'd say, 'Holy shit. Are you stupid or what? You can't smoke around the kid. Now your kid's in ICU. It's. A. Big. Deal. The kid could die. So three strikes you're out and a relief pitcher is coming in. The kid will be going home with another family. One that won't try to kill her. End of story.' Next."

Margo raised her eyebrows and gave a short laugh. "Ah. Well, points for honesty, but perhaps you need to tone it down just a little. Put yourself in the mother's shoes and ask 'what if.' What if she's trying her hardest? What if she tried to change, cut back, smoked outside? Maybe the child has other triggers. What can you do to help the mother be successful? Smoking cessation counseling, nicotine replacement, parenting strategies. It may be that she's so stressed about the child that she's smoking to calm her nerves."

"But what about the kid? Who's advocating for her?"

"Good point. You are. Ultimately, keeping families together is really in the best interest of everyone. Unless there's abuse or neglect. That's a different story. But if the mother is willing and able to make some changes, she should be given the chance."

Trace didn't look convinced. "Okay. So bottom line, at least find out what the mother's perspective is."

"Yes. Keep in mind you don't have to feel empathy to show it." Margo continued to roll the paint on the wall. "What if the child dies in the ICU and the mom gets angry and claims the care was substandard?"

"Then I think it would be fair to point out the mother's role in this. Her smoking, how long it took her to bring the child in . . ."

"Think about it though. Her child has died. She's angry."

Trace sipped his coffee. "So the anger isn't exactly a lawsuit brewing. It's a mother's grief."

Margo turned and pointed at him. "Exactly. The slightest suggestion that the mother's at fault could make it worse. Much worse. Can you imagine the guilt that would sit on the mother's shoulders if you suggested she killed the child by smoking? And for what? The child's dead. Don't do it. It's cruel."

"What if she did it on purpose?"

Margo shrugged. "I guess there's a whole spectrum of possibilities. But that would be for the courts to decide. Our job is to help her heal. As much as we can."

"So what would you say to her?"

"I'd say, 'I'm sorry your child has died. Everything possible was done to try to save her.'"

"That's it?"

"That's it." She dipped a brush in the paint and stood on the stool to paint the edge at the top. "Okay, next scenario.

"A thirty-six-year-old truck driver comes in for a physical exam to renew his driver's license. He has epilepsy and hasn't had a seizure for seven years – until three weeks ago. He was partying, celebrating his wife's pregnancy, and forgot to take his medication. The next day he had a seizure. He doesn't want you to write it down because he'll lose his driver's license for a year. He needs it, especially now with the baby coming. He swears he'll never forget his medication again. What do you do?"

"Put myself in his shoes. You gotta feel sorry for him. A bun in the oven, his livelihood on the line. I'd have to say I'd side with the dude and pretend he never told me."

Margo nodded and rolled the paint on the wall. "The following week he's driving on the highway, has a seizure and causes an accident, killing three people, one of them your Aunt Teresa."

Trace jerked back with a wince. "Shit. Not Mother Teresa. Harsh."

Margo shrugged. "Empathy isn't about avoiding harsh decisions. It's about supporting patients when those harsh decisions come down the wire."

"So you tell the dude that you have to write it down and watch all hell break loose."

"Pretty much. Make sure that it's fair and necessary in your head and then try to explain it. In this case, the law states that you have to disclose the information. So the decision is out of your hands. But it doesn't make it any easier to tell the patient."

"What would you say to him?"

"Tell him that you don't have any choice, you have to write it down. Apologize. Brainstorm possible solutions with him. Offer to advocate for him. Get him seen by a neurologist to assess whether his condition is changing. Stay calm while he vents."

"Basically sit by helplessly."

Margo smirked. "Pretty much, yup." She turned and looked at him. "Although it surprises me how much better patients feel when their feelings are validated. Knowing that someone commiserates with them is often help enough."

"Misery loves company?"

She tilted her head. "Yes. But more, we acknowledge that it is a rough go, and other people in their situation would also find it difficult."

Trace nodded.

"K. Here's another. You're a surgeon."

Trace's face lit up. "Always wanted to be a surgeon."

Margo laughed. "You operate on a three-year-old child to remove a mass. During the operation, the specimen is sent to a pathologist and you're told it's cancer. Immediately following the surgery, you tell the parents. Obviously they're devastated. The next day, the pathologist calls you and tells you that now that they've had a chance to look at the sample more closely, do further testing, and consult another pathologist with more expertise, they've determined that it's benign. It's not cancer." She paused. "What do you do?"

"Call the parents with the good news."

Margo nodded.

"Apologize and explain," he added.

"Good. Say they're angry for putting them through hell, would you lay the blame on the pathologist?"

Trace thought for a moment. "Be hard not to. But no. They're doing the best with what they've got. But it might change the way I do things. Like wait until they're sure."

"Yes, very good. You're a team. You shouldn't diss

the team members. It's done and no good will come of it. Apologize and thank the stars that the result didn't go the other way." Margo dipped the roller in the paint. She turned to raise an eyebrow at Trace. "More?"

"Yes, but let me get some cereal and another coffee. Do you want anything?"

"Any of those muffins left?"

Trace pointed to the container still sitting on the island counter. "Help yourself. I'll get you a plate. Coffee?"

Margo shook her head. "Just the muffin."

Trace returned with a bowl of Cap'n Crunch cereal and a plate for her.

Margo set her brush down and walked over to sit on the stool at the island. "Aren't you too old to be eating sugar for breakfast?"

"Breakfast of champions." He grinned with his mouth full.

"All part of your strategy?"

"You bet." He scooped another mouthful. "Okay, ready. Hit me."

Margo smiled and split a muffin in two. "A couple comes into your office together for the results of the husband's physical exam and tests. They're told that the husband has a neuromuscular disorder and the outlook isn't good. A week later the wife calls and asks you to write a letter outlining the disabilities so they can get the ball rolling for some insurance money to renovate their home." She paused. "Do you write the letter?"

Trace swallowed. "Yes. Poor bloke. I want to do whatever I can to help," he said confidently.

Margo nodded. "Turns out the wife wants to divorce the husband and uses the letter in court to prove he is incapable of looking after their children. She wins sole custody."

"Holy shit. What?"

"True case. The doctor was sued for providing a letter without the patient's written consent."

"Even though the wife was at the visit and knew it all anyway."

"Even though. Confidentiality is a big deal. You can't let on what you know, or even say if a person is a patient, without their permission." She popped a piece of muffin in her mouth. "And no discussing details in an elevator or at the coffee shop. Eavesdroppers are everywhere."

"It's a mine field. How do you figure it all out?"

Margo finished the muffin and brushed the crumbs to the center of the plate. "Some of it's common sense. Being humble helps. And respectful. Once you've had patients who trust you with their stories, you appreciate what a gift it is to be able to help them." She gave a crooked smile. "That probably sounds a bit hokey."

He smiled at her. "I'm using feng shui. Get in the hokey pokey line behind me."

She laughed and wondered what it would be like to wake up beside those twinkling blue eyes. "I better get back to work." She stood up.

"This is really helpful. Is this what you were asked when you applied?"

She shook her head. "This is stuff I saw during my clerkship. Sixteen months of seeing patients."

"Wow, a lot of shit goes down. Got any more?"

"Unfortunately, yes." She picked up the paintbrush and stepped on the step stool to touch up the edge by the ceiling. "A twenty-two-year-old male comes in asking for a renewal of his asthma medication. He states that he's been asthmatic since he was little, but the vague history is out of keeping for someone living with asthma for years. You know that the inhaler device has a street value. It can be sold and used to inhale street drugs. You wonder if that's how this prescription is going to be used." She stepped down and picked up the roller. "Do you write the prescription?"

"What if he truly is asthmatic?"

"He could have an acute asthma attack and die without the medication."

Trace frowned. "Damned if you do, damned if you don't."

Margo smiled and nodded.

"I think I'd go with trusting what he says. His dying seems a bigger risk. And it wouldn't look too good on my CV."

"It's frowned upon," she agreed. "That's what I did, too. I suppose I could have called his pharmacy, but he was visiting from out of town, and I didn't get a gut sense that he was lying. I could've been wrong, but the doctor-patient relationship is built on trust, and at some point you have to trust that the patient isn't lying to you."

Trace nodded as he finished the cereal.

"How about this," Margo continued. "What would you do if you saw a resident using cocaine at a party?"

"A resident is a student?"

"They have their medical degree and are working toward a full license to practice. Often they see patients on their own, but technically they're still supervised."

"So snorting cocaine would be frowned upon, as you say."

"Yes."

"And it's pretty unlikely that they would only snort once, so something should be done."

"Yes. I've not been in that situation, but I think I would report it. They obviously need help. And a cocaine-using doctor is a very scary combo, any way you look at it.

"When you're applying to medicine, they love to throw these ethical dilemmas at you. And often there's no right or wrong. They want to see how you think, how you approach the problem. They want to see that you can be nonjudgmental and empathetic."

"Right. So consider what it's like to be in the other person's skin. Show them I get it. Ideally they should leave feeling better. And keep everything confidential," he said.

"Exactly."

"I should be good at this." He grinned. "Sounds a lot like foreplay."

Chapter 10

Margo folded the last of the drop sheets and packed them neatly in her tote bag. She threw the rollers, tray liners, and two empty cans of paint in a plastic trash bag.

Trace had a weekend tutorial to run for some of the first-year students and had left after lunch, which turned out well. Without him to distract her, she powered through the rest of the job and finished it. Even the baseboards got a touch-up and it was only four o'clock. She wouldn't say she rushed it at the end, exactly. But if she could get cleaned up and out the door before he returned, she would call it a good day.

Foreplay indeed. She suppressed a shiver. He definitely thought outside the box. And it was a very sexy box.

But it was also Pandora's Box to her, and the sooner she was out of there, the better.

She wrapped the brushes to take home to clean and stuffed them in a side pocket of the tote. She swept the floors and put the stool back in the closet where it belonged. All done. It would take a couple of trips to load her car. She shrugged on her coat and found the keys in her pocket just as the door to the condo opened.

Her heart skipped a beat when Trace walked in.

He stopped when he saw her all packed up. "Leaving so soon?"

"All done."

He came closer and she smelled the fresh outdoor air on his jacket.

"Beautiful."

She looked around at the smooth blue of the walls. For a

pale color, it exuded strength and calm. She'd have to agree. She'd done a good job. "Thanks. I think it looks good, too."

"I didn't mean the walls," he said.

She raised startled eyes to his but looked away at the intensity of his gaze. "It'll . . . It'll just take a couple of trips to clear this stuff out," she stammered.

"I can help you," he said.

She passed him the totes, and when his hand lingered on hers, felt a flutter of panic. Can't go there. Shouldn't go there, her mind raced. It was a guaranteed one-way street to heartache.

With her head down, she pulled back and then picked up the half-empty paint can and the rest of her gear. Trace held the door open, and they walked down the hallway to the elevator.

They stepped in silently when the doors opened.

18

17

"So tomorrow you start another job?" Trace asked.

She nodded. "Another residential, on Savior."

16

15

"Thanks again for getting it done this weekend. How much do I owe you?"

A lifetime of forgiveness. "Don't worry about it. I'll send you a bill."

He nodded.

She watched the numbers count down. The elevator was slower than the average green van.

14

13

12

"So, how often are you at the soup kitchen? What did you call it? The Breakfast Table?"

She smiled. "Breaking Bread. I usually try to go twice a week, on Tuesdays and Thursdays. Depends on my schedule, though. They're pretty flexible and can always use a hand."

He nodded. "Right. Breaking Bread." He nodded again.

11

10

9

8

"I'll be working on my application to medical school this week. Can I get in touch if, you know, I need advice?"

7

6

"Sure."

5

4

"I'm on Facebook," she said reluctantly. "Send me a friend request."

"You know, they say you shouldn't accept a friend request unless you'd be willing to go out for a beer with the person."

"Really?"

"Yup." He shifted the totes in his hands. "Maybe we should test that out."

3

"Ask all our friends if they'd be willing to go out for a beer with us?" she asked.

2

"Starting with us. Would you like to go out for a beer with me?"

Her heart sank as she saw how she walked into that one. Heartache. Heartache, her brain screamed.

1 Ding. The elevator doors opened.

"Friday, if you're free. I have to write a bunch of short essays for the application. Why don't we meet, and you can give me your expert opinion," he added when she didn't answer.

She looked him in the eye. And was ashamed to see the hurt there. "I'd like that," she said finally.

He grinned. "Great. Seven o'clock. O'Malley's. Their burgers and fries are the best in town."

They arrived at her Mini Coop. She popped open the hood of the trunk and stowed the paint can inside. "I guess I'll see you Friday then?"

He nodded, set the totes in the car, and then leaned forward and brushed his lips gently against hers. Her breath caught at the touch and her eyes fluttered closed. "Thanks for all your help," he said quietly.

She opened her eyes and looked at him. It was a moment before she could speak. "You're welcome."

He opened the car door for her. "Drive safely in this little rat-trap. Don't want you skidding all over the road."

Her eyes widened. How dare he criticize her beloved Mini Coop. "You don't drive a green van, do you?"

He looked pained. "Please. A van? Seriously?" He shook his head. "I'm hurt that you think so little of me." He closed her door.

She laughed and rolled down the window. "You insulted my Coop."

"Only because I care."

She started the engine.

"See you Friday," he said with a smile.

She couldn't help smiling as she pulled away and rolled up the window. He was cute. But what kind of car did he drive?

Chapter 11

Margo pulled open the back door of Breaking Bread and with a flourish of cold air, stepped inside.

She was a bit late. Not that anyone checked their watch when she arrived, but she had wanted to be there in time to help prep the meal.

She would have been even later, except that she managed to get in behind a white sedan. She followed him closely as he blew through three yellow lights. The lights hadn't turned red by the time they passed the intersection, so it was legal. Sort of. And it shaved a good six minutes off her twenty-minute drive. Meaning she was only four minutes late. Bonus.

She unzipped her jacket, hung it on a hook near the door, and rubbed her shoes on the mat to dry off. It was damp outside, but the snow hadn't stayed on the ground. Surprisingly. It was later than usual. Hopefully they wouldn't catch up with a granddaddy of a storm.

She pulled a hair band from her pocket, quickly twisted her hair up out of the way, and walked through to the kitchen.

"Margo, honey. How are you?" She was enveloped in a big hug. Hattie was a staple at Breaking Bread. A large woman with a booming voice and ready smile, she was there most days to organize the crew. Nothing really started until Hattie said it did. Just don't ask her to do the washing up. Shopping, slicing, dicing, peeling, cooking, serving, she didn't have a problem with. She'd even stay late to put everything away. But washing and drying were off the list.

Margo couldn't even recall why, but knew enough not to hand Hattie the dishrag.

"I'm great, Hattie. I meant to be here a bit sooner. Do you have a job for me?"

Hattie laughed and her shoulders shook. "We've always got a job for you, honey." She handed her a carrot peeler. "Here you go. If you thought coming late would get you out of cleaning carrots, you'd be wrong."

Margo laughed. "Do you need them cut, too?"

"Not today. Thought we'd have a nice carrot and raisin salad. We'll shred them and Jimmy there is making the dressing. It'll go with the leek and quinoa soup and fresh rolls."

Margo gave a wave to Jimmy across the kitchen. "Sounds delicious."

"Hey baby girl, thank you for sending Barbara Crombie our way. She was in yesterday, and boy can that woman stretch a vegetable. She says you been talking up Breaking Bread, and she came to pitch in."

Margo smiled as she peeled the carrots. "I'm so glad it worked out. She's a fabulous cook and a mom of six."

"And has more than a few tricks in the kitchen. And she don't mind washing up neither."

"Bonus," Margo said. Hattie would welcome anyone to help, but it was nice to send her someone who made a difference.

"Carl's out there today."

Margo nodded. "Okay. I'll give him a chance to eat and then go and see him."

Margo finished peeling the carrots and hauled out the food processor. She pushed the carrots through until a big bowl was full of shredded carrot. "Here you go, Jimmy. Ready for the dressing."

Jimmy tossed the carrots with chopped red onion, a bowl

of raisins, and the dressing, then set the bowl out, ready to serve.

Hattie stirred the soup and grabbed a spoon to taste. Throwing a bit more pepper in, she deemed it done and transferred the pot to the edge of the serving table. Baskets of rolls with tiny pats of butter, a basket of bananas, and empty bowls with a canister of spoons and knives filled the table.

As Hattie rounded up the guests for dinner, Margo filled the sink with hot water, squirted in the dish soap, and added a dash of bleach. On their wish list was a dishwasher. For now, she was it. She started with the cutting boards and knives and washed down the counters. As the guests finished their meals, the bowls were rinsed and added to the sink.

"Take a break honey, and go see about Carl and his meds," Hattie reminded her.

"Will do." She peeled off her dish gloves and left them hanging on the edge of the sink.

It always helped if she gave Carl a choice between orange juice and water, so she poured a glass of each and carried them through the swinging door into the dining room.

Eight rectangular wooden tables filled the room. The dark polished wood was an elegant contrast to the paper flowers sitting in colored glass vases at each table. Hattie had a knack for getting the community to pitch in.

A local high school tech class had built the tables, sanded, and then stained them a rich mahogany color. The vases were old wine bottles that a glass artist salvaged, and the flowers were the artwork of the grade one class whose school was right next door. The six chairs around each table, in a mish mash of styles, were donated over the years. Margo had taken the worst and painted them. Some were a solid color and some told the story of a guest. It became their chair, in their spot, and welcomed them to the table. And heaven help ya if you decided to sit in someone else's coveted chair.

Margo walked over to Carl, who sat in his usual spot across from Angie, the rest of the table empty. Carl looked a little worse for wear with a scruffy beard, an old torn flannel jacket, and greasy hair under a black tuque.

He smiled when he saw her, but his eyes quickly shifted back and forth between her and his two bags of belongings under his chair.

She smiled at Angie and then sat down beside Carl. "Hi, Carl."

"Hi, Doc. You're not gonna take my stuff are you?"

"No, not at all. I brought you juice and water to take with your pills. Which do you want today?"

"Juice."

"Here you go." She handed him the juice and set the water down in front of her. "Have you been taking your medication like we discussed?"

"Yes. Every day with dinner like you said."

She nodded. "That's good. Have the voices been quiet?"

He swallowed a pill and nodded vigorously. "Only heard 'em once or twice. You're not gonna take my stuff are you?"

"Nope. I just came to say hello and see how you're doing. Where're you sleeping?"

"The shelter. They've been letting us stay a little longer with the cold outside."

Margo nodded. "That's good. And have you been showering at the Y?" She wondered how Angie could sit so close with the waft of his body odor.

"They said they've been having a problem with their hot water. Told me to come back on Wednesday. But I was thinking of waiting 'til Friday in case the poison's not out."

"I wouldn't worry about that. If they say it's safe on Wednesday, it'll be safe."

"Are you sure? I don't want no poison."

"Yes, I'm sure. Are you still working at the market for Mr. Rebel?"

"He didn't need me yesterday, so I'm going to go back after I can get to the shower. But I was waiting for the poison to clear."

"Do you want me to check with the Y and see if they got it fixed? Maybe you could go tonight and then get back to work tomorrow?"

"Okay. If you think the poison is gone . . ."

"I'll call and find out. In the meantime, it's important to take your medication every day. Even when I'm not here, okay?"

"What if they try to poison me?"

"You can trust everyone here, Carl. We wouldn't let anyone poison you."

"Okay."

"I'll go call now." She got up and turned toward the door, idly scanning the rest of the room and then stopped, staring.

Blond hair. Broad shoulders.

Trace? What was he doing here, sitting with Ottie?

Ottie was an eighty-year-old spry little guy with an unwavering toothless grin, oversized round glasses, and a black top hat. He looked like he was having an animated discussion with Trace, but stopped and lifted his top hat in greeting when she stared.

Trace turned to look and added his wave to Ottie's greeting. Margo walked closer.

Ottie stood as she approached. "Hello, Doc. Delicious meal you made tonight. The carrot salad is my favorite."

Margo smiled. "I'm glad you liked it." She turned to Trace.

"The soup was divine," he said with a twinkle in his eye.

Before she could comment, he continued. "I came to serve, but Ottie here mentioned he's a Shields fan." He shook his head sadly. "That's when I knew my true calling was not in service, but to turn Ottie toward fan enlightenment."

Ottie chuckled.

"We can't have him pining for a win from the Shields. He'll be doomed to disappointment," Trace added with a mock shake of his head.

Ottie pulled out a sticker for the Cascades. "He thinks I should stick this on my top hat. Change to the dark side."

Margo smiled at Ottie's wide grin and small round face, the top hat covering most of his forehead. "It would definitely start a fashion trend. There'll be a run on the sale of top hats. All the fans will want one."

"Maybe I ought to find a Shields sticker. I've been rooting for them for eighty years. Can't change it up now despite this whippersnapper's advice."

"Don't let him sway you, Ottie. You could teach *him* a thing or two," Margo said. She gave him a wink.

Ottie's grin cracked the wrinkles of his face and he let out a hoot. He tipped his hat. "Making mistakes is the best teacher."

"Then he'll be an A+ student," Margo said.

"Hey." Trace laughed as Ottie bent over laughing.

"Don't keep him too long, Ottie. The dishes are waiting."

"And we gotta stay on Hattie's good side. I'm hoping for ice cream on Friday."

Margo laughed. "I'll let her know. I'll see you later in the week."

Ottie tipped his hat and grinned.

She turned to leave and heard them both laughing as she swung into the kitchen.

She called the Y and let Carl know it was okay to go back and then pulled on gloves to wash the dishes stacked to the side.

A few minutes later, Trace walked in, carrying another load of bowls. He set them down beside her and picked up a dry tea towel.

Margo looked over at him with her hands in the soapy water. "Fancy meeting you here."

He grinned. "I'm trying to reach out and find my empathy."

"How's that going?"

"Pretty good. I could put myself in Ottie's shoes. He's got a cool top hat."

She laughed.

"But I also learned that he misses his friends, most of whom have kicked the bucket. His wife has Alzheimer's and doesn't recognize him, and his only daughter died of cancer last year."

"I didn't know about his wife and daughter. He's lonely," Margo murmured.

Trace nodded. "But he's an avid hockey fan and follows all the games on a small radio he carries around. He's cheering for the wrong team, but he knows hockey."

"He probably appreciates sharing it with you. Not many stop to chat with him about it."

"Yeah. It felt a bit awkward grabbing some soup, but it felt even more awkward sitting there and not eating with him."

Margo nodded. "Breaking bread with others is what it's all about. Nobody minds."

"Good to know. Ottie's a special guy."

So are you. Not many would stop to sit and chat. It was easier to hide in the kitchen. She stacked another bowl in the rack for him to dry. "Their stories can be heartbreaking, but they smile and carry on."

"You have to admire them." He dried a bowl and set it on the counter. "And the soup was delicious. Mrs. Crombie was here yesterday. She had a ball."

"Really? Hattie said she appreciated her help."

"Do you recruit everyone you meet?"

"Pretty much."

"Glad to see there aren't any other boyfriends here," Trace said, tongue-in-cheek.

Margo laughed and shook her head. She finished the last bowl and handed it over to Trace.

Hattie came bustling into the kitchen. She put the bowls away and cleared off the counters. "Looks like we're all done here," she said, looking around the room. "Thanks for all your help. It goes a lot quicker." She looked over at Margo. "We'll see you Thursday?"

"Yes, ma'am. I'll be here as soon as I can, after work."

"Thanks, darlin'. I sure do appreciate it. How about you, honey pot? Will you be back?" Hattie asked, looking at Trace.

Trace nodded. "I promised Ottie I'd take him to watch the game tomorrow. So I'll come and help out and then take him over to the pub."

"That's mighty fine of you," Hattie said.

"I made him a bet that the Cascades would score the first goal. If they do, he has to wear the Cascade sticker on his top hat. If they don't, I'm supplying ice cream all next week."

Hattie's laughter filled the air. "Butterscotch ripple. That's all I'm gonna say 'bout how that'll turn out."

Trace smiled. "Ottie's sure of a win if there's butterscotch ripple on the line?"

"Exactly." Hattie pulled out her keys as they put on their coats. "You two have a wonderful evening. I'll lock behind you and then head out the front door in the dining room to double check it's locked."

Trace held the door open for Margo, and when it closed, they heard the click of a lock.

Margo pulled out her scarf and wrapped it around her neck, tucking the ends in her jacket. "Brrr . . . feels colder."

"Wanna come and warm up at Decker's? I'm meeting a few guys for a beer," Trace asked with a persuasive smile.

"Will Daniel be there?"

Trace's smile dimmed. He stuck his hands in his pockets and looked away. "I don't know."

Margo winced. "I didn't mean–"

"No, it's fine. I get it," he interjected. "Mutual admiration. I'm not sure which of the boys will be there. The text goes out. Whoever shows, shows."

Margo shifted her purse on her shoulder. "Oh. Of course. Look, I'd better not. I had a busy day today, and tomorrow is an early start. Thanks for the invite, though."

"Yeah, no problem. We're still on for Friday?"

"Yup. You're going to bring the answers to your essay questions?"

Trace looked at her. "I've been chewing through them. They'll be done by Friday," he said with false cheer.

"Great. I'll see you then."

He paused. "Would you like me to pick you up?"

"That's okay. It'll be easier for me to meet you at O'Malley's. I'll be out and about anyway."

"Okay, then. I guess I'll see you on Friday." He reached behind her and opened her door.

Margo held her breath when he moved toward her and released it on a sigh when he reached past. "Do . . . Do you want a ride?"

He shook his head. "Nah. I'll walk," he said with a shrug. "It's not far and the cold air will do me good. Drive safe." He closed her door for her and stepped back with a wave.

As she started the car, she watched him walk away, his hands in his pockets and his shoulders hunched. Her stomach churned. *Good job, Margo. Way to make someone feel bad.* What was wrong with keeping it professional? She couldn't get involved with him. She couldn't go there. She sighed as she watched him in the shadow of the streetlight. Too late.

Chapter 12

Margo watched the snow fly. The flakes were falling softly and melting as they hit the ground. Time for snow tires, Margo thought.

She wondered if the little blue hatchback even noticed. He slid to a stop when the light turned red and then fishtailed out of the intersection with the green. *Time for some winter driving lessons, buddy.* And a few lessons on safe lane changing wouldn't hurt either. What was it about blue car drivers? Was it a blue hatchback sin to stay in one lane for more than a three-minute stretch? Maybe they were all a little paranoid and needed a reason to be constantly looking over their shoulder.

She accelerated to get out of the hatchback's blind spot and turned into the parking lot at Breaking Bread. She was a little earlier today. With Chloe's help, the second coat of paint at their current job had gone on quickly, and they had to take a break so it could dry. She was out the door by three o'clock and had time to go home, have a bite to eat, and change.

It was three forty-five when she pulled open the back door and walked in. Margo slipped off her coat and hung it up.

"Hey, baby girl. Come on in out of the cold." Hattie stood at the stove stirring an enormous pot.

"Something smells delicious." Margo leaned over the pot and inhaled the spicy steam. "Three bean soup?" she guessed.

Hattie wrapped her free arm around Margo's shoulders and gave a squeeze. "That it is. Three bean soup with corn bread." She winked. "And butterscotch ripple ice cream for dessert."

Margo laughed. "I saw the goal. It was a good one."

A grin split Hattie's face. "Ottie is very happy. He's asking for dessert first."

"He could eat a full meal, and he'd still have room for butterscotch ripple."

They laughed together and Margo got to work setting out the dishes and preparing the table for the buffet.

"He's a nice boy, that Trace. I think he's got his eyes on you. He's mighty interested in your schedule."

Margo hid her wince. "He is a nice guy. I'm helping him apply to medicine."

"Are you now?" Hattie turned to look at her with a surprised glance.

Margo tried not to blush. "I don't know how much help I'll be, but he asked–"

"Of course you'll be helpful. Who better to ask? Does all that revisiting put you in a mood to try it out again?" Hattie had never hid what she thought of Margo's decision.

"Not so far."

"We can always hope. Speaking of medicine, Ottie's been complaining about his ear again."

"I could take a look. I could bring the otoscope in next week."

"I was hopin' you'd offer. I snagged the otoscope and ear syringe from the clinic tonight before they closed. I told 'em I'd bring it back tomorrow, but they was happy to lend it. It's there on the counter."

"Perfect. How much time until dinner?"

"Twenty minutes. He'll be bustin' happy if you could help him hear again."

"Let me talk to him." Margo picked up the otoscope, walked into the dining room, and glanced around. The room was starting to fill up, but she saw Ottie in his usual chair. She made her way over and as soon as he saw her, he grinned, stood up, and tipped his hat.

"Did you hear we're having butterscotch ripple?" he asked.

She laughed. "I did. Well played."

He smacked his lips. "I can't wait. Trace was as good as his word, taking me to the game, and stocking up on ice cream after the first goal. And he's never without a smile. I like him."

Margo smiled.

"And he slipped in the odd question or two about you. Real subtle. Not too pushy."

Margo's eyes widened.

"So I told him what I know. I think he's all right for you. Better if he was a doctor. You don't want a bum. But he's pretty sharp with all that fancy math stuff. I think he would work out."

Margo choked out a laugh. "Good to know. I'll keep it in mind. Hattie mentioned that your ear is bothering you," she said quickly to change the subject.

He put his finger in his right ear. "Can't hear out of this one. Good thing we watched the game at the pub. No way I could listen to it. I think it might be the wax again."

"Come with me, and I'll take a look."

"I'd appreciate that." He followed her to a small room off the kitchen.

She put the otoscope to his ear. "You're right, it's wax."

She syringed it out with warm water, and Ottie let out a sigh of relief when his hearing returned. "Thank you very much. I was beginning to feel a little crooked with my ear blocked like that. Wow, that is some improvement." He wiggled his head. "Thank you. Sure is handy having a doctor at the dinner table. One stop shop."

Margo put a hand on his shoulder. "I'm happy to help. Bean soup with corn bread tonight."

"Oh, I'm looking forward to it. And to the butterscotch ripple," he added with a wide grin.

"Enjoy your meal, Ottie."

He went back to the dining room, and she cleaned up and went to help Hattie serve.

At the end of the evening, with the dishes done and stacked away, Hattie turned to Margo. "You have yourself a wonderful weekend. I hope your plans include some fun. Maybe some fun spelled T-R-A-C-E," she said with a wiggle of her eyebrows.

Margo smiled weakly and slipped her jacket on. Another matchmaker, just like Ottie and Mrs. Crombie. Did they get together on public transit and plan? Discuss how other people should run their lives between stops?

Oh well, it could be worse. They could be yellow car people.

Chapter 13

This was supposed to be fun. She kept telling herself that. She pulled on jeans, a long-sleeved dark purple shirt, and a sweater splashed with bright flowers.

She looked in the mirror at the dark circles under her eyes and smeared on another layer of make-up. Fun. Her hair curled around her face. The snow had stopped, and the air was dry, so at least her hair wasn't poufy. She left it down and hooked dangling pink and purple earrings in her ears.

What could be more fun than meeting up with the one person who, if they really knew you, would have nothing to do with you?

She sat down on the edge of the bed. She really needed to spruce up the color in this room. It was such a downer. Maybe she should buy a gallon of bright pink, with the energy and happiness of a five-year-old girl. That would liven things up. Of course, then she might not be able to fall asleep.

She sighed and picked up her black leather ankle boots, carried them into the living room, and set them down by the front door.

This room was better. The walls were gray with an undertone of blue in the light. But it was the blast of color in her collection of artwork that really pulled her in. A collection of six square photographs in substantial black frames hung above the sofa – colorful blossoms with the energy of spring. Her own painting, an abstract in blues and greens with a hint of orange, hung on the opposite wall. She routinely changed the cushions on the sofa and right now, in winter, tried to infuse the warmth of the sun with a splash of red and orange. Black piping mimicked the frames on the walls and added to the symmetry. She found the color energizing rather than soothing, and that usually worked for her.

She shrugged on a black jacket, tied a red scarf around her neck, and slipped her feet into the boots. Checking for her keys, she headed out.

She had planned to drive, with the intention of delivering some artwork to a client who lived close to the pub. But as the week wore on and her mood went down, she decided alcohol might be helpful to make it through the evening. So Plan B, walk. It wasn't far, probably only twenty minutes or so. But the temperatures had dipped and the sidewalks were icy, so instead she moved to Plan C and waved down a taxi. She sat back in the warmth for the short drive.

O'Malley's was hopping. Some patrons sat, some stood at the bar with a beer in hand, eyes glued to the television screens. As she made her way across the bar to the tables in the back, the crowd cheered in unison. She dodged the jovial backslapping, squeezed past the revelers, and spotted Trace in a booth off to the side.

He stood as she approached. "Where was that on Wednesday night?" he asked looking at the screen.

Margo laughed as they took a seat across from one another. "I heard Ottie got his butterscotch ripple."

"He was gleeful. He can do a fine little jig when he's excited."

"I bet he can. Ice cream's a precious rarity."

Trace nodded with a grin. "Would you like a beer?"

"Anything light would be great."

Trace caught the waitress' attention and ordered for them both.

Margo looked at the stack of papers. "You've been a busy bee."

"When someone tells me something is due tomorrow, I generally figure I can do it tomorrow. If it's math. It's going to take a little longer to wade through all of this, I think." He paid the waitress when she set down the drinks.

Margo took a sip of her beer. "Show me what you've got."

He picked up the top sheet of paper. "This is a spreadsheet with the five schools I'm applying to, the questions they want answered, the maximum number of words required, and the due date."

Margo raised her eyebrows. "Very organized."

"Thank you." He pulled out the next pile of papers and removed a paper clip. "The questions are similar but just different enough to be annoying. Here's the most comprehensive." He handed her four typewritten pages. She read them slowly.

Why do you want to be a medical doctor?

I have wanted to be a doctor from a young age. Doctors can be very influential and can positively affect someone's life. When my grandfather passed away last year, his encouragement and insight made me realize how much I would like to strive for this goal.

I may not be the best at medical research, but I am very interested in it and feel that I could contribute to the analysis and methodology of many studies.

There are a wide variety of jobs within the medical field and this appeals to me. I particularly like helping people.

Should medical doctors have higher moral standards than construction workers?

Yes, doctors have access to private information and need to keep it private. Construction workers don't have the same privileges or have the need for the same level of professionalism.

Describe an experience where you showed collaboration.

When I tutored, I had to work with each student and determine their unique way of learning to develop a strategy that would be most effective. We worked together to find a time to meet, which was sometimes quite difficult when we both had busy schedules. We would have to determine their individual needs, figure out what they didn't understand and come up with a plan to help them learn the material. This was often time consuming. Ultimately, the students really appreciated the time I took and seemed to improve in their learning.

What qualities should every physician possess? Which qualities do you have? What do you need to work on?

Physicians should be smart, compassionate, dedicated, good listeners, good at giving advice, and involved in medical research.

I am smart, dedicated, interested in people, and fairly good at listening. There are many medical research papers with flawed statistical analysis and that is an area where I excel.

I'm working on empathy but feel that it is within my reach.

Margo finished reading. *First, do no harm.* She looked at Trace. He sipped his beer and watched the screen across the room. He leaned back with a smile when the bar erupted in another cheer. And then noticed her watching him.

"That bad?" he asked with a lopsided grin.

"No. You're answers aren't bad." She frowned. How honest should she be? "They're good. Not excellent, but they would do."

"I don't want mediocre. I want to get in."

Okay then. Brutally honest. "I know. I know." She took a sip of beer. "You've answered the questions, but you've really just scratched the surface. Two things are important.

"First, the focus should be on you. Specifically, what have *you* done with respect to the statements you've made? You say that doctors can be influential. What happened to make you realize that?" The crowd cheered again. Margo glanced over at the screen and tried to explain. "A hockey coach wouldn't recruit a player without knowing the player had talent. They'd want to see that dedication on and off the ice before they signed him. Same thing here. You need to convey in your answers your specific experience to show how you've prepared yourself for a career in medicine, how you can handle the rigor of the curriculum, and how you've worked to develop interpersonal skills. You've thought about it, you've taken steps to make sure you know what you're getting into, and because of that, you know medicine's a good fit. Specifically, for you."

"Skip the royal 'we', stick to what I've actually done," Trace repeated with a lift of his eyebrows.

Margo nodded. "Yes, exactly." Margo picked up the napkin and wiped the condensation off her drink. "Second, you should ask yourself why they're asking the question. How does it relate to the qualities they're looking for in a doctor? The question about the construction worker may be about ethics. Or about being judgmental. Who knows? Collaboration is all about communication skills, teamwork, leadership, time management. In your answer you need to address the qualities and again relate it back to you."

"Hold on." Trace flagged down the waitress and flashing a smile, asked if he could borrow a pen. The waitress produced one with an equally interested smile, and ignoring Margo, walked away with an exaggerated sway of her hips. Trace grinned appreciatively when Margo smirked.

"Okay, I'm going to write this down. One, focus on me. That shouldn't be too hard," he said with a grin. He made a note on his spreadsheet. "Two, the doctor perspective. What else?"

"Do you want more?" she asked hesitantly.

"Yes. Lay it on."

She sighed. "Let's go over each one. First question. Your

reasons are good, just add more specific examples. And don't put yourself down."

He nodded and made a note.

"Two. Stating that construction workers don't have the same level of professionalism is judgmental," she said. "You need to change that. Discuss why doctors need to have high moral standards. Give an example where you've had a reason to keep something confidential, respected someone's decision, advocated for human rights, whatever. Make it about you. Then speak to when construction workers would also have to have high moral standards. Point out the differences, but the bottom line is the basic human need to be treated well.

"Question three. You need an introduction. You taught math at the undergrad level so many hours a week. Details. Relate how your tutoring has prepared you for a career in medicine."

Trace scribbled and then looked up at her. "Because it helped with communication skills?"

"Yes, but what specifically?"

"Showed I like working with people. That I can adapt how I teach something to different styles of learning."

"Yes. Good. And patients come with varying levels of literacy, understanding of English, and desire to learn. You have to explore all that and make sure, at the end of the day, they understand what you're saying. In medicine and in math."

"Got it."

"You can add you honed your time management skills, and worked for a team. Did you ever have to advocate for a student?"

Trace thought for a moment. "Twice, actually. Once to challenge a grade and once to support a deadline extension."

She nodded. "Perfect. That's part of collaboration."

Trace tapped the pen and then made a note. "Advocacy. Relate to medicine." He looked up expectantly.

"Fourth one. Add examples. Be brief. Be concise. Take out the diss about medical papers. We don't like team members who stab us in the back. And remove you're working on empathy. You're going to master that before your interview." She looked at him pointedly and he grinned. "Whenever you're asked for a weakness, you need to come up with a weakness that's actually a strength."

"What?"

"Yes. Selflessness can be detrimental to you, but ultimately good for society so that's a good one. Whatever you choose, always mention you recognize it as a weakness and the steps you're taking to improve."

"K. What else?"

"One trait that would be good for you to mention, is that doctors have to be lifelong learners. Your interest in research would be a good example of that because ultimately you'll be contributing to the ever-changing face of medicine."

Trace wrote it down and tapped the pen. He raised his eyebrows at her.

She smiled. "I think that's everything."

Trace leaned back. "Whew. That's a lot. No wonder I didn't get an interview last time. Here I thought I did a good job."

"You did. But this will up the ante to excellent."

The crowd cheered again, and they both glanced over at the screen.

"To winning," Trace said as he tapped his mug with hers. "And to not giving up." He watched her over the rim of his mug as he took a sip.

Chapter 14

Margo tried not to squirm. She gathered up his papers and handed them back to him without a word.

She ignored the speculative look in his eyes as he folded them and stuffed them in his jacket.

"Hey, do you snowboard?" he asked.

Margo looked at him, startled. She'd been sure he was going to razz her about medicine. "Yeah, I do."

"A bunch of us are heading to Massif next weekend, if you'd like to come. I think Dan's coming, so it won't be all dummies like me. There'll be some smart people for you to hang out with, too."

Margo snorted. "When are you leaving?"

"Probably Friday afternoon. I think we'll try to pack everyone into two cars. If we leave about three, we should be there by six and can get some night boarding in. Jess Preston has a ski in, ski out with lots of space."

"That sounds really fun. If you're sure she won't mind me coming along."

"No, she's cool. I'll send you a message on Facebook when we sort it all out."

"Great. Thanks." She swirled the beer at the bottom of her glass. "Trace?"

He looked her in the eye. "Yes, Margo," he said with a smile when she didn't say anything.

Those blue eyes were seductive. "Last I heard, you had to be very smart to get through a master's degree in math," she said.

He nodded slowly. "I don't know about smart, but you definitely have to be calculating."

Margo laughed. "And witty."

"Possibly wise," he added.

"Sounds infinitely better than smart."

"When you put us all in the same room, we add up to something. We can get to the root of a problem. And we love pie."

Margo grinned. "Maybe I should start hanging around mathletes more. They sound like a fun bunch."

"We are, we are. It's an exclusive group, but any time you want to hang out, you let me know."

"Will do." She finished her beer.

Trace nodded at her glass. "Want another?"

Margo hesitated. "No, I'd better not. I should get going."

"Big plans for the weekend?"

"I'm meeting up with a friend of mine. Mikaela and I went through medical school together. She's in the midst of an obstetrics and gynecology residency."

"Now there's something I wouldn't want to do."

"Me, either," Margo said with a laugh. "But she loves it. She has this weekend off, so we're getting together tomorrow night."

"Girl time."

"Exactly. I'm just going to call a cab," Margo said, pulling out her cell phone.

"Let me. I'm cabbing it, too. I can drop you off and then continue on to my place."

"It's a bit out of your way."

"No problem." He called and arranged for a cab to pick them up.

They put on their coats and headed outside. The restaurant was quieter now with fewer people to dodge at the bar.

When the taxi reached her apartment building, Trace got out with her and walked her to her door. "Thanks for all your help with the questions. Can I get you to look them over after I make the changes?"

"Sure. Email them or bring them to Breaking Bread. I'll be there Tuesday and Thursday."

"Perfect. Thanks." He leaned in and hesitated. Margo knew she could move away. But she didn't.

He brushed his lips against hers and teased her lips open with his tongue. Margo's skin tingled from head to toe, and she stepped in to press against him. Too many layers. His tongue never stopped moving. She shivered as he moved down the curve of her neck. Oh, to go lower.

He eased back and kissed her lips one more time. "The taxi's waiting. I should go. But I'll be in touch about next weekend."

Margo's eyes fluttered open, and she swallowed. "Next weekend. Sure."

Trace flashed a smile and jogged off to the waiting cab. She watched him go and then walked to the elevators, half floating on air. Her breasts felt heavy and a delicious stirring swirled in her belly.

She had one week to buy condoms.

Chapter 15

Margo balanced a pizza in one hand and knocked on Mikaela's door with the other. She knew Mikaela wouldn't mind if she walked right in, but Mikaela would never have such lax security. She adjusted the strap of her overnight bag on her shoulder and pulled her coat edges together. Were winters getting colder or did she need to invest in a better coat? She stamped her feet to get the worst of the snow off as Mikaela opened the door.

The waft of warm air and Mikaela's welcoming smile drew her in. "Hey, stranger. Come in. Long time, no see." Mikaela gave Margo a hug and reached to take the pizza.

"You talking about me or the pizza?" Margo asked. She set her bag down and hung her coat in the closet. She heard Mikaela's laugh in the kitchen and followed her there.

"Both." Mikaela opened the lid to the pizza box and inhaled deeply, watching the steam rise. "Mmmm . . . smells delicious. You got Hawaiian," she said with grateful eyes.

"Of course. Wouldn't want to split up a perfect friendship."

"Ours or the pizza's?"

"Both," Margo said as they laughed.

"You, me, pizza, and wine. Go together like a bath and a rubber ducky."

"So true. Perfect on their own but so much more fun together."

Mikaela cut them each a slice while Margo poured the wine. They sat down at the table and dug in.

"Delicious," Margo said, eating a strand of cheese. "So

what's new in the world of a first year ob-gyn resident?"

Mikaela looked relaxed in sweatpants and a warm sweater. Her glossy straight brown hair hung down to her shoulders. Even with the glow of perfect skin, dark circles under her eyes had become a permanent fixture since the start of her residency seven months ago. "Let's see. What have I learned?" She wiped her mouth with a napkin. "I'm in the fertility clinic this week. It's pretty specialized so I've mostly shadowed my preceptor. But he has a lot of pearls."

"For instance . . .?"

"An egg only lives for twenty-four hours, but sperm can live for seventy-two, so if you want to conceive you need to have sex three days before you ovulate."

"Good to know. I'll keep that in mind for better birth control."

"Yes, it works both ways. Also, the elevating-the-bum-with-a-pillow-after-sex rumor may actually have some merit."

"Increases the chances of a meet and greet?"

Mikaela grinned and took a sip of her wine. "Yes, exactly. Although no evidence that keeping your legs in the air or doing a handstand works."

"I'll stop practicing my handstands."

Mikaela nodded. "Informative and time-saving." She smiled. "Also, this just off the press, swallowing sperm cannot get you pregnant."

Margo snorted. "Seriously? Some creative guy's wishful thinking?"

"Apparently. And half the population really liked that one, so why dispel the myth?"

"You should start a blog."

Mikaela laughed. "In my spare time. How about you? What's new in the world of painting? I couldn't believe you worked last weekend," Mikaela said with wide eyes. "What was that all about?"

"Got an offer and the bank was very happy I took it." Margo shrugged. "Turns out it was Brett Bennett's son."

"Really? Is he as cute as his dad?"

"Better. Icy blue eyes, gorgeous smile . . ."

Mikaela wiggled her eyebrows. "Built?"

"Built."

"Oooh. Sounds serious. Does he have the ass factor?"

Margo took another bite of pizza and chewed it slowly. Finally she swallowed. "A great ass? Check. A bit of badass attitude? Check. A piece of my heart?" She wiped her mouth with a napkin. "Maybe."

Mikaela set her pizza down. "Name," she demanded.

"Trace."

"Trace. Trace Bennett. Trace Bennett with the ass factor."

Margo tried not to blush under her friend's pointed stare. "I said maybe."

"But it wasn't a 'no'. I think this is a first." Mikaela raised her glass of wine. "To Trace Bennett with the ass factor. May I hear more stories about him in the future."

Margo gave a small smile. "His grandfather is, was, Ernie Pearce."

Mikaela set her glass down with a clunk and wine sloshed onto the table. "What?"

Margo nodded.

"No. Trace Bennett with the ass factor is connected to all that?"

Margo nodded.

"Does he know?"

"No."

"Are you going to tell him?"

Margo gave a large sigh and swirled the wine in her glass. "I don't know. I think it would be better, and save a lot of heartache, if I just walked away."

"But he has the ass factor."

Margo smirked. "I'm hoping there's someone else in my future with the ass factor."

Mikaela shook her head. "I'm so sorry, honey." She reached over and squeezed Margo's hand. "Don't relive the whole thing."

"I know. I'm trying not to."

"If there's anything I can do . . ."

Margo shook her head. "Sharing pizza tonight is a good start. May need another bottle of wine."

Mikaela smiled gently. "Why don't you talk it over with him? Explain it."

Margo grimaced. "I should. I know it. But I'll feel like a failure all over again. He's asked me to help him with a medical school application. I'm doing it, sort of like penance." She looked at Mikaela. "Hoping it will balance the world energy of karma or something."

Mikaela frowned. "You don't need to do penance or . . ." She waved her hand in the air. ". . . worry about cosmic energy. You didn't do anything wrong. You gave some old guy hope. What was so wrong with that? It was a good thing."

"I gave him false hope. There's a difference."

"You were a student. You weren't the only one talking to him."

"He told me things he didn't tell the others. And my words had impact. He'd have done things differently if I'd kept quiet."

"Maybe. Maybe not."

Margo shook her head and her curls bounced wildly around her face. "I don't want to discuss it. I know you think it was perfectly reasonable, and I appreciate it. I really do, but I still carry the burden of it all. I can't go after the ass factor."

"But it's the ass factor. Your first," Mikaela said with regret in her voice.

"I know. Pass the wine."

Chapter 16

Margo was up to her elbows in soapy water when Trace walked in carrying a stack of bowls.

"Hi, when did you get here?" she asked. Not that she had been keeping track. But he hadn't been in the dining room when she set out the soup. Or put out the napkins. Or rearranged the cutlery. When she gave Carl his orange juice or Ottie his ice cream. Not that she had been keeping track.

He grinned. "Just stopped by. The Shields lost last night to the Cascades, so I thought I'd come by and keep Ottie up to date."

"Rub it in, you mean."

"As he sat polishing off a bowl of butterscotch ripple. I think that eased the pain."

Margo chuckled.

"Actually, I was hoping to catch you here," said Trace, as he picked up a tea towel and started drying dishes.

Margo's heart skipped a beat. She didn't trust herself to speak.

"I finished the revisions to my essay questions, and I was hoping you'd look them over."

Margo's shoulders relaxed. "Of course. Hattie had to leave early tonight, so let me go wipe off the tables and lock the front door. Then I'll take a look." She set the last of the bowls in the drying rack and grabbed a clean wet cloth for the tables.

Trace worked his way through the cutlery and bowls until Margo returned. She walked back into the kitchen carrying two dirty spoons. She threw them in the sink of soapy water and finished wiping down the counters in the kitchen.

When it was all sparkling clean, she turned to Trace. "Okay, let's see."

Trace handed her the papers and continued drying as she read.

Why do you want to be a medical doctor?

I want to be a doctor because I'm interested in pursuing medical research. A friend died of cancer at age fifteen, and I realized how much more there is to learn about the cause and cure of cancer. I have focused my undergraduate studies on math and biochemistry to have a solid foundation for analyzing and understanding medical research. A medical degree would allow me to pursue this further and with greater impact.

I have extensive experience tutoring mathematics to undergraduate students and thoroughly enjoy interacting with people and adjusting how I teach to how they learn. As a doctor, I would be able to do the same with patients.

I have given a great deal of thought on the future path of my career. My major goal is to do what I can to use my skills to help others. I am excited at the opportunity to dedicate my life to a career in medicine to fulfill this.

Should medical doctors have higher moral standards than construction workers?

Medical doctors and construction workers need to have high moral standards.

Doctors are privy to very personal information. It is very important that they keep the information confidential, have a respectful, nonjudgmental relationship with patients, be honest, and work well as part of an interdisciplinary team. They are role models for health and professionalism. They are trusted to make decisions, which can significantly affect the health and well-being of their patients.

Construction workers need to have high moral standards in their work for public health and safety. Using inferior materials or cutting corners may have devastating results.

Regardless of the job, whether I'm tutoring a student or volunteering at Breaking Bread, a soup kitchen, I feel it is very important to treat others with dignity and respect. I've done this by being punctual, maintaining confidentiality, speaking respectfully, and doing the best I can. These are all qualities that would be essential for a physician.

Describe an experience where you showed collaboration.

I spend approximately fifteen hours a week tutoring mathematics to undergraduate students. I have never had any difficulty in school, and I believe it is very important that I use my skills to help others. In particular, when I meet with students, they are often stressed and upset, and it is satisfying to see them gain some understanding of their subject and succeed. A focus of my tutoring strategy is to tailor the teaching to the student. It is not only important to understand what the student struggles with, but also to determine the unique way each student learns. I present the material in a number of different ways – using different language, approaches, or analogies – so that each student can understand it. I think this skill will prepare me for interacting with patients. Medicine involves relating to a wide variety of people and teaching them about their health in a way that they can understand.

Tutoring provided valuable experience in advocating for students when their marks were incorrect or the amount of effort was questioned. I felt it was important as a leader to take on this responsibility.

I had to manage my time wisely to balance tutoring with completing my course work. Knowing that I could handle both will help me with the rigorous medical curriculum.

What qualities should every physician possess? Which qualities do you have? What do you need to work on?

Physicians should be smart and committed to lifelong learning. They should enjoy working with people and have excellent interpersonal skills including listening and giving information in a clear, nonjudgmental way. They should be passionate about health and comfortable with making decisions in a high-pressure environment.

I have maintained a high GPA throughout four years of undergraduate studies and have finished a combined major in mathematics and biochemistry. This consistent performance and my desire to focus on medical research, demonstrate that I am hardworking and committed to lifelong learning. My extensive tutoring experience has honed my interpersonal skills and demonstrates that I can listen and adapt to specific needs. Through tutoring and my position on the Venn Group, I have shown leadership. I was awarded two competitive scholarships after performing well at high-pressure interviews.

I get caught up in work that I find extremely interesting but also want to find the time to participate in basketball and hockey. Finding a balance would be important.

I have given a great deal of thought about the future path of my career. I strongly believe that I am an excellent candidate for medical school and am excited at the opportunity to be dedicated to medicine for my entire life.

Margo looked up and caught Trace watching her. He raised his brows.

"Wow," she said.

Trace broke into a huge grin. "Really?"

"Yes." She nodded emphatically. "This is excellent. It's focused on you. It relates your experience to the qualities of a physician. It's thoughtful and well written. I really like it. Great job, Trace."

"Thanks." He swept her up in a hug. "Thanks." He looked down at her, his eyes intent.

Margo held her breath and then stumbled back out of his embrace. "One . . . One more thing done," she stuttered. "What's left? I guess your references. Have you decided who to ask? You'll need three, I think, right?" *Margo, stop talking*, she chided herself silently.

Trace folded the papers and put them back in his coat pocket. "I was thinking of asking my master's supervisor. He's recommended me to students to tutor so he could cover that. The head of the Department of Math said he would write a reference, and I've had a few courses with him so he can comment on my marks. I wasn't sure about the third one."

"Have you done any medical research? Worked on stats for anyone?"

"Yes. I did some number crunching for a prof in immunology. Calculated the minimum population size needed and then analyzed the data after. Just basic chi-square and regression analysis. She was going to include my name on the paper, but I don't know if it was ever published," he said with a shrug.

"Either way, it would be perfect. Could you ask her?"

"I think so. She was pretty grateful for the help."

"Excellent. Make sure you give them lots of time. It's done electronically, but . . ."

"Yeah. I think it's just a matter of giving them a link and then following up to make sure it was done."

"And some guidance from you as to why you've chosen them. Don't forget to thank them after."

"Yes, Mom," Trace said with a laugh.

Margo rolled her eyes. "Sounds like you've got it all under control. I really hope it works out for you."

"Yeah, me too. Thanks for all your help."

"You're welcome." Margo looked around the room a little desperately. "Well, it looks like we're done here. I promised Hattie I'd lock up and then drop the key off at her place on my way home. Do you need a ride?"

"No. I'm fine. I'm going to head out for a brew. It's a business brew. A couple of buddies have an idea for a start-up and asked if I could look over the numbers for them."

"Wouldn't they need an accountant for that?" she asked.

"Depends how many beers they've had."

Margo laughed, and Trace watched her with a smile.

They put on their coats and headed outside.

"Did you see the message about Friday?" Trace asked. "Jess is driving, and we can pick you up at three. That work for you?"

Margo's stomach churned with second thoughts. "Are you sure I won't be in the way? It sounded like a full house, and I wondered if you still wanted me to go?"

"Yes, I definitely do." Trace stepped closer. She could feel his warm breath in the cold air. "I'd like you to come. It'll be fun. And I'll get a chance to thank you for helping me with the application." He leaned in and pressed his lips to hers.

He tasted sweet, and her heart swirled in her chest.

"Three o'clock. Friday. Okay?"

She nodded and sighed. Friday. Fun.

Then heartache.

She'd pencil that in.

Chapter 17

Margo shook her head at the shiny gray jeep stopped beside her at the light. The shiny gray jeep with no doors. She'd seen it in the summer, but with temperatures a few degrees above freezing, she'd want doors. He didn't seem to mind. With a tuque pulled down over his ears, a multicolored scarf blowing in the wind, rosy cheeks, and his thumbs tapping on the steering wheel to the hard rock bass blaring from his speakers, the driver looked pretty content. He glanced over and smiled, and Margo couldn't help smiling back. You had to love those free-spirited drivers of no-door, shiny gray Jeeps.

He accelerated when the light turned green, and Margo pulled away more sedately. She was meeting Chloe at a residential address and was a bit early.

She pulled into the driveway of the massive two-story house and waved to Chloe who was arriving on foot. Chloe had her bleached-blond hair pulled back in her usual ponytail. She looked warm in a lime green jacket with a yellow scarf wrapped around her ears and neck. Chloe waved back and hurried over as Margo stepped out of her car.

Margo held out the tea she had picked up at the drive-thru. "Tea for you."

"Oh, thank you. I love the walk to work, but the cold is starting to seep into my bones. This tea will hit the spot." As they walked to the front door, Chloe cracked the tab and took a sip. "Mmmm . . . perfect. Thanks." She pulled a key out of the oversized handbag she carried. "The owners have gone away for the week, so we can blitz the rest and get it done." She slipped the key in the lock and pushed open the door. "Go ahead."

Margo looked around at the walls of the front hallway as she slipped off her coat. "Good job here, Chloe. Much as I love color, you can't go wrong with your basic Frost on Glass white."

"I know. It always looks so fresh and clean," Chloe said, slipping off her coat and hanging it on the banister. "I finished the bathrooms, living room, kitchen, and one bedroom. I prepped the walls for the master and the two other bedrooms, so it's just the painting left."

"Perfect. We should be able to get it done today and tomorrow. What color have they chosen?"

"White, white, and more white," Chloe said.

Margo raised surprised brows. Sounded like the homeowners planned to sell. "Makes it easier."

Chloe sipped her tea and nodded. "The bedrooms are all upstairs. I'll show you." She led the way up a curved staircase, down a hallway, and through a set of double doors to the master bedroom. The furniture, pushed to the center of the room, had been covered in plastic, and the curtains and rods had been taken down.

"Looks good. Let's get started," Margo said.

With the ease of a routine developed over working together for six months, Margo picked out a brush to do the edging. She pried the lid off the paint can, dipped a stir stick in, and swirled it around.

Chloe prepared a paint tray and slid a new sleeve on the roller brush. "You were quick at the Johnson place."

"It wasn't as big as this job. They added a family room and changed the study into a baby's room. She's expecting twins," Margo said with a grin.

"No. Really? How does Neal feel about that?"

"Looks a bit shell-shocked," Margo said. "But happy.

They both seem really happy. I think they've lined up most of their relatives to help them in the first few weeks."

"When's she due?"

"Any day now. I was happy to finish up. I haven't delivered a baby in a while, and I wasn't keen to practice."

"Do you miss it?" Chloe asked as she rolled the first coat on.

Margo shrugged. "Sometimes. Some parts. Some parts I don't miss at all."

"I'd miss it."

Margo laughed. "How do you know?"

"How can you not? You're a doctor. It's not a regular Joe job. All that doctor knowledge floating in your head, going to waste. Doctor blood flowing through your veins. Don't you feel like reaching out and helping someone every day?"

Margo looked over at her with surprise. "Absolutely. That's why I'm here now. You need help. I'm helping."

Chloe shook her head. "No, really. Like doing CPR at the library. Delivering a baby in a taxi. Removing someone's appendix."

Margo snorted. "Sounds very glamorous."

"Yes. That's it exactly. It's so glamorous. How can you give that up?"

Margo focused on making the edge clean and straight. "It's not all popcorn and cherry blossoms. Sometimes it's heartbreaking and . . . hard."

Chloe dipped the roller brush in the tray and rolled off the excess paint. "Sure it is. That's why they call it M.D. . . . mucho difficulto. That's why you get the big bucks."

"What if it's not worth the money? What if it's too hard?"

"I suppose you need to suck it up, buttercup, as my mother would say. Life is hard. Doesn't mean you give up. Look at me. I want a baby, and I thought I was all set. Life with Roger was breezing along. Life was good, and then, bam. He up and tells me that he doesn't ever want kids. Not,

I might not. Not, I'm a little scared of the little rugrats. Nope. It was a big emphatic NO. It was a deal breaker. Good-bye Roger. Was that difficult? Yes. Did I give up? No. I'm going to have a baby."

Margo looked over. "Really?"

"Absolutely. They may have to squirt the little swimmers in with a turkey baster, but it's going to happen. You can't always stick with white paint, you know? Sure it's safe and reliable. But sometimes you need to throw a little color in the mix."

Margo dipped her brush in the white paint. Good advice, but she liked safe and reliable. Painting was easy. If you messed up, chose the wrong color, painted outside the lines, you painted over it. No fuss. No guilt.

Medicine was different. It never seemed to be white. It was a stormy gray, oil on acrylic, can't reach behind the toilet, splotch on a new hardwood floor, kind of job.

Her shoulders sagged. But Chloe may be right. She needed color. She just wasn't sure how much.

Chapter 18

A black Suburban. Margo should've guessed. Jess 'flawless skin, not an ounce of spare fat, smoky eyes,' Preston drove a honking big black Suburban. Cause that's what you needed to get to your mega mansion ski chalet every weekend. She probably had a matching ski ensemble and was comfortable in a thong. Who was comfortable in a thong? People like her, that's who.

Margo sat in the back of the Suburban, sharing the seat with snowboarding boots, helmets, suitcases, and her sleeping bag. That was embarrassing. Did ya bring a tent, too? Trace had teased her.

What? She did laundry. She knew it was a hassle washing all the sheets after the guests left. She thought a sleeping bag was a good idea.

Well, apparently not. Jess looked down her nose. A silk duvet and 800 thread count sheets weren't good enough? By all means, bring your sleeping bag. Lots of room in the Suburban. They threw the sleeping bag in, and she crawled in beside it for the ride.

Only three hours. Seemed really short when she thought about it on Wednesday. But half an hour into it, and she'd already had enough of the 'isn't the air up here in our social stratosphere so much cleaner' banter between the Hustler and Dick Trace in the front.

Daniel was driving the other two in their party of six. He had a sporty Jeep. With doors. How come she wasn't in the sporty Jeep with doors? How did she end up riding in the suburbs with the luggage?

Margo sighed and checked her watch again. Thirty-two minutes down. Only one hundred and forty-eight minutes to go.

Trace twisted in his seat with an expectant look.

She would not blush. She was not the town idiot. Smart people daydreamed. "Sorry?" she asked.

"I said that Jess is applying to medicine this year, too."

"Oh, wow. Good luck, Jess." Really? Hoping to steer people to the correct facial cream?

"Thanks. I'm interested in neurosurgery," Jess said, looking at her in the rearview mirror.

Of course.

"I was telling her how much you helped me with my application, that you could make a business of it," Trace said with an encouraging smile.

Margo smiled weakly. One hundred and forty-two minutes.

"Oh, actually the dean of medicine is a really good friend of Daddy's. He said he would give me a few pointers," Jess said.

Of course. Because that's the norm for thong-wearing beauties who drive black Suburbans.

Margo looked out the window and watched the snowflakes fall as they chewed up the miles.

At least she and Chloe had finished the painting. She would have felt worse if she'd left Chloe to clean up, for this. But they had been done and out the door by lunch, and she'd had plenty of time to pack. Lots of time to dig out her sleeping bag. Thank goodness for that.

Jess and Trace laughed in the front seat, and she frowned.

Why was she here? She rubbed her stomach as the burning pain flared. Why did he invite her? He's obviously pretty tight with Miss Hand Cream for All. They laughed again. All she got was the 'make me sound good on paper' conversation and the 'why aren't you in medicine?' stink eye. How come Suburbababy got all the flirty eyes and sexy chuckles?

She sighed. One hundred and thirty-eight minutes.

"Not enough air back there for ya?" Trace asked as he twisted to look at her.

"What?" Margo asked.

"All that heavy sighing. Sounds like you're having an asthma attack." He laughed. "Good thing there's a doctor here."

Margo stifled a sigh. And forced a smile. Should have packed inhalers with the sleeping bag.

They made it to the chalet. Glorious three-story, six-bedroom Tudor on the side of the mountain. Lit up like a Christmas tree, all neatly shoveled, and hot chili waiting on the oven. The smell of warm garlic bread filled the air.

Suburban people weren't all bad.

They unpacked the cars and threw their suitcases and duffel bags in the bedrooms. Margo snagged a room next to Daniel, one floor above and a long hallway away from the rooms Trace and Suburbababy chose. If they were going to be doing the horizontal rumba, she didn't need to hear the bed-squeaking beat.

They scooped bowls of chili, added salad and warm garlic bread, and spread out on the main floor. Margo joined Daniel and Hannah at the giant antique wooden dining table. Trace and Matt sprawled on the leather sofa in front of the crackling fire. Suburbababy was still freshening up. A games table, and two recliners flanking a sturdy reading lamp, filled out the rest of the main floor.

There was easy chatter, with the occasional crack of the wood splitting in the fire, as they filled their stomachs and relaxed.

Margo learned Hannah was Jess's roommate at school. Poor girl. She had invited Daniel. Mmmm.

"Anyone up for night boarding?" Trace asked.

Jess came down the stairs, elegant and glowing in a pink cashmere sweater and figure-hugging yoga pants. Not a hair out of place. No underwear lines. "I can't, unfortunately. Last weekend I twisted my binding on a half pipe. I left my board at the shop, and I'll have to pick it up tomorrow morning. But you go ahead. I'm going to settle in with a glass of wine and enjoy the fire."

"I'm out, too. I'll stay and keep Jess company," Hannah added.

Not that she was a huge fan of night boarding, especially on the first ride of the season, but it came down to staying in the chalet with Suburbababy or getting out there and risking her neck on icy, unknown terrain. "I'm in," said Margo.

Not surprising, all the boys were in. XY equals risk taking. She hadn't forgotten everything from med school.

The temperature had fallen below freezing with the setting sun, so they layered up and laced on their boots.

"What are you doing?" Trace asked as he watched Matt spray his goggles.

"Anti-fog spray. It really works."

"Really? I thought you were supposed to use toothpaste," said Daniel.

"Isn't that for a scuba mask?" Hannah asked.

"Put your goggles on in the chalet and don't take them off in the gondola. That's what works," said Trace.

Matt shrugged. "I've heard using the hand drier in the bathroom works too, but I've always used the spray."

"Sounds like you need new goggles," Trace said, patting Matt on the back.

They walked out the front door and down a short path to the slope. They threw down their boards and strapped into the bindings.

Trace looked over at Margo. "You're goofy-footed?" he asked with a grin.

Margo looked at the three of them. All regular. Figures. "Right-brain dominant," she said.

They hopped with their feet strapped into their boards the few steps to the hill. The ride down was a quick ten minutes. The lower section was well lit and an easy run.

Margo brought up the rear. The conditions were a bit icy, but snow was falling. They'd have fresh powder in the morning. She shifted her weight to slow down and slid into the line for the gondola. Unstrapping her bindings, she carried her board onto the gondola with the others.

Trace traded insults with Matt with the ease of a long friendship. Daniel gave as good as he got as they bantered on the ride up. The gondola slowed and they hopped off and strapped on their boards.

They had time for three runs before the gondola shut down for the night. With the last run, they headed across the slope toward the chalet.

Margo leaned into the curve and listened to the scrape of her blade as she carved back and forth. She'd love to let go. Just fly. But she couldn't see more than ten feet in front of her. She missed a bump and almost caught an edge on a rut. She'd had her share of face plants in the past, but tonight she decided to take it easy and stay upright. She swung into the landing of the chalet and smiled at Matt's exuberant woohoo. He felt the rider's high.

She couldn't wait for tomorrow. Sunshine and fresh powder, it was going to be great.

Chapter 19

Margo stood at the top of the mountain and tucked her mitten back into her sleeve. Jess, Matt, and Hannah had peeled off for lunch, but she stayed with Trace and Daniel to do one more run from the top. They hadn't made first tracks in the morning, but even getting out at 10 a.m., they'd had fresh powder and plenty of runs.

She raised her chin to catch the warm sun. Blue skies, cold, but not fingertip numbing temperatures, and fresh air. Couldn't ask for a more beautiful day.

"Coming?" Trace asked. He threw her a smile and leaned into the run. Margo glanced at Daniel who smiled that he was ready to go.

She gave a little jump, twisted to line up her board, and edged forward. What a rush. It was so effortless cruising down the hill carving a big S, frosty wind on her cheeks. And Trace in her sight. Not a bad view all round.

She shifted her weight and changed direction. Her board chattered under her feet and she tensed and bent at the knees. Rippling ice? She watched her edge, but it didn't feel icy. She felt the grip and let it go again. She looked up to watch Trace shredding down the hill.

As they rounded a bend at the edge of the forest, a young skier, crouched low and flying straight down the hill, blew past Trace. Trace instinctively pulled back, caught an edge and launched five feet into the air. He raised his arm to break his fall against a tree and landed with a splash in the snow.

Oh my God, Trace. Margo's heart pounded as she carved toward him and came to a stop with a spray of snow off the board. She leaned down, snapped off her bindings, and raced over. "Trace. Are you okay?"

He was lying on his back in the snow. "Fuck. Where the hell did he come from? Fuck."

"Are you hurt?"

"My shoulder."

Daniel raced over to join them. "What happened?"

"He was cut off by a skier. Flew through the air and hit the tree," Margo explained. "Did you hit your head, Trace? Any neck pain?"

"No. Dammit. My shoulder stings like a bitch, though."

"The left?"

"Yeah."

Margo tore off her gloves and unzipped the top of Trace's jacket to feel his arm.

"I dislocated it playing basketball two years ago. Feels the same," Trace managed through gritted teeth.

She knelt beside him and palpated his shoulder. No pain along the clavicle. Prominent acromion, abnormal contour of the shoulder. No pain along the humeral shaft. "Can you feel this Trace?" She brushed the skin of his upper arm with a light touch.

"Yes."

She checked the pulse at his wrist. Weak and fast, but present. "There's a good chance it's dislocated again."

Trace nodded.

"I could try to reduce it," Margo said, watching beads of sweat form on Trace's brow.

"No. It's too risky. If it's fractured, you'll make it worse," Daniel argued. "I've called for help. They patrol this area. We should just wait."

"But the quicker it's reduced, the better the outcome. He's had a previous dislocation. He's young. It'll help with the pain," Margo said, as Trace winced.

"I think you should wait," Daniel insisted.

Trace looked at Margo. "Can you do it?"

"I could try. Daniel's right about a fracture, though. There is that risk."

"Go for it."

"Really?"

"Yeah. I trust you. Do it."

With shaking hands, Margo gently grasped Trace's arm and flexed it ninety degrees. Trace clenched his jaw.

"Try to relax." Slowly, she applied force as she externally rotated the shoulder. Sweat dripped down her back. At sixty degrees, she felt a clunk as the bone moved into place.

Trace let out a breath with a groan. "Better."

"Can you touch your right shoulder with the left hand?" Margo asked.

Trace slowly moved his hand toward the shoulder. "Yeah. It feels better." He looked at her. "Thank you."

Margo nodded. "Rest your arm at ninety degrees. They'll put it in a sling." She zipped up his coat. "Are you cold?"

The roar of a snowmobile filled the air.

"I'm okay."

The ski patrol pulled up and after a quick assessment, they immobilized Trace's arm. They shifted him to a stretcher and covered him with a blanket.

"We'll meet you at the bottom, Trace."

As they pulled away, Daniel turned to her. "That was a fool move, Margo. You could have made it worse."

Margo stared at him. "But I didn't."

"You were lucky. I wouldn't have done that without an x-ray. With a history of trauma, you couldn't rule out a fracture."

"I examined him."

"With his coat on. In the middle of ski slope. Less than ideal conditions."

"Maybe. But if his pain increased, I would have stopped.

The risk was pretty low. Pain equals shock and early reduction lessens disability. You know that."

"How many of those have you done?"

Margo was silent.

"None? You've never done that?"

"I've seen it. Isn't that how it's done in medicine? See one, do one, teach one." She put her hands on her hips.

Daniel shook his head. "You don't even have a license to practice medicine. You should be more careful. The next time you might not be so lucky."

Margo turned away and slipped her goggles over her eyes. She picked up her gloves and retrieved her board. With shaking hands, she tightened the bindings. Pointing her shoulder in the direction she wanted to go, she crouched and let it go.

Tears worked on foggy goggles, too.

Chapter 20

An ambulance waited at the bottom of the hill. Margo rode as close as she could, then unstrapped one foot and skated over.

"I don't think I need to go to the hospital in an ambulance. It actually feels a lot better," Trace told the paramedic.

"Trace, you should have your shoulder x-rayed," Margo said and released her other foot.

Trace looked over and grimaced. "Really? Couldn't it wait? I'm sure my parents will want me to see a doctor in Rivermede."

Margo hesitated. It probably could wait, but Daniel had her rattled. "Why don't you go for the x-ray here? They can always send it electronically to a specialist in Rivermede. That won't be a problem."

Trace sighed. "All right. Whatever. Can you come?"

Margo glanced at the paramedic, who nodded. "Sure."

Daniel skated over and lifted his goggles off his face. "What's going on?"

Margo stayed silent. Trace looked from her to Daniel and then spoke, "I'm going to the hospital for an x-ray. Margo's coming with me."

Daniel nodded briskly. "Good idea. I can take the boards."

The ambulance ride to the hospital was short, and Trace was whisked away to a room. After a few minutes, a nurse told Margo she could join him and showed her to his room.

Trace was sitting on a stretcher in a hospital gown, texting, and frowning.

Margo walked in, and he looked up.

"This is such a waste of time," Trace complained.

Margo shrugged. "Maybe, but it's better to know." She took a seat in the chair in the corner of the room. "It was an impressive jump. The landing needs a little work though," she said with a small smile.

Trace snorted. "We need boarder-only hills."

"Beginner snowboarders are just as bad. I hear skiers complaining about them all the time."

"True. Not sure how that kid got on a double black diamond, though."

"*He* made it down safely," Margo said tongue-in-cheek.

Trace laughed. "Maybe I should go back to the green runs."

The emergency room doctor came in. He was a big, burly man with a quiet voice. Trace told Margo to stay when she started to leave.

The doctor asked about the accident and performed a thorough physical examination. Trace winced at the extremes of movement of his arm, but otherwise was pain-free.

"Was it subluxated? Popped in and out?" the doctor asked.

"No, it was out." Trace nodded to Margo. "She put it back in."

The doctor turned to Margo with a raised brow. "Really? Good job. The quicker you get these back in, the better. Looks good now. We'll get an x-ray to check the position, and put it in a sling, but you should be good to go. Sling for one to two weeks, physio for a few more. No sports until it's healed completely, probably ten to twelve weeks."

Trace nodded. "Okay. I'll arrange that at home. Thanks."

The doctor wrote down the instructions and gave Trace a prescription for painkillers.

Soon after, Trace was taken for the x-ray. When the

result came back normal, he turned to Margo. "See, waste of time."

Margo made a face. "It helps us sleep at night."

Before they left the hospital, Trace checked his phone and scowled. "It's a dislocated shoulder. You'd think I'd broken my neck." He looked at Margo. "My mom wants me back in Rivermede."

"She's probably worried."

"Yeah."

"Is she coming to get you?"

"Not exactly." He gave her a sheepish look. "She's sending the chopper."

Margo laughed. "What? A helicopter?"

"Yeah. I have to be at the airport in twenty minutes. They've got a small window to land and hit the air again."

"I'm surprised a town this size has an airport."

"Apparently it's not too far out of town." He shook his head, exasperated. "We can grab a cab back to the chalet and drop you off, and then I'll head to the airport. What a pain."

Margo shrugged. "You can't snowboard, and it'll be more comfortable than three hours in a car." Three hours with Suburbababy. Or silence with Daniel. *Any room for her in that chopper?* She glanced at her watch. "I don't think we'll have time to return to the chalet first. We can go to the airport, and I can get to the chalet from there."

"Sorry about all this," Trace said.

Margo smiled. "Are you kidding? Reducing dislocations and delivering patients to helicopters is all in a day's work."

Trace laughed. "Let's go. It'll probably take longer to find a cab than it did to arrange for the chopper."

They made it to the airport as the helicopter landed. Margo asked the taxi to wait and helped Trace through the gate. He was waved out onto the tarmac while the blades whirred overhead. The pilot stopped him, gesturing about his arm and they huddled with their heads together, talking.

Suddenly, Trace turned toward Margo and gestured for her to come.

Margo pointed at herself and raised her hands to question it. Trace started to walk over, but the pilot brushed his shoulder and indicated he should wait.

The pilot jogged over. "You're a doctor?"

Margo raised her brows in surprise. "Yes."

"Can you come with us? I know it's a shoulder dislocation, but as a rule, if it was severe enough to warrant a hospital visit, I shouldn't be in the air without a medic. Can't fly a chopper and save a life at the same time."

"Cool. I'd love to go," Margo said.

Trace had already settled the taxi fare, so she told the driver about their change of plans and raced out to the helicopter.

"I'm so sorry about this, Margo. It ruins your weekend," Trace said with sad eyes.

"Not at all. This is fantastic. I've always wanted to fly in a helicopter. This is so awesome." She grinned from ear to ear. "Not that I would have wished a dislocated shoulder on you, but as silver linings go, this is pretty shiny."

Trace laughed and sat back in his seat.

Margo enjoyed the weightless feeling as the helicopter lifted, dipped, and flew toward Rivermede. The view, oh the view. Lots of white snow. Blue frozen ponds. The ridge of mountains dotted with ski lifts, opened into stretches of flat fields. Tiny houses with smoking chimneys. The highway looked like a stream of moving ants on a gray ribbon. She recognized Rivermede as they flew overhead. The buildings were denser, the parking lots bigger. Her heart beat to the rhythm of the blades as they followed the edge of the lake toward the airport. She must have been a helicopter pilot in another life. The ride was way too short.

Margo spotted the limo waiting on the tarmac as the chopper started to descend.

Shit. Of course his parents would meet him. His mom was anxious enough to send a helicopter.

Margo had met his dad many times in the course of business. He was a nice guy. She liked him. She had met his mom only once, briefly, when she had to break the news of her father's death. Margo's heart beat faster as the chopper blades slowed. Yeah, the ride was way too short.

Chapter 21

Margo slammed on the brakes as the Hummer cut in front of her. She was tempted to lean on the horn, but by the time she thought of it, the Hummer had sailed across two lanes of traffic and beat the rest of them through the yellow light. An orange Hummer, no less. Big honking box of steel in a neon wrapper. No need to learn the rules of the road. Not when you drove a flashing orange, make way, step aside, I'm coming through, Hummer. At that moment, she wished she had one.

Margo tapped her thumbs on the steering wheel. Why did red lights always seem longer when you were running behind?

She wondered if Trace would show up at Breaking Bread. He hadn't missed a Tuesday, but he also hadn't been recovering from a dislocated shoulder.

She had declined his offer of a ride home from the airport. It turned out his parents hadn't been there, but the reality of it all came crashing down, and she knew she had to cut the ties. If she could find someone with sexy eyes, a disarming smile, and that hormone-hopping pull, without all the heart-wrenching history, it'd be golden.

And single. Single would be good too. She didn't want someone with a back-up girlfriend in the wings. She couldn't compete with no-underwear-line Suburbababy.

A car honked and Margo jumped. *Oops. Green light.* She gave a guilty look in the rear-view mirror and accelerated with a jerk.

She pulled into the parking lot at Breaking Bread and turned off her car. She took a moment to zip up her coat and pull her hat over her ears. It was a short run to the door, but the air was icy cold. The day had been gray and damp, and the temperatures dropped even further with the setting sun.

"Hello, honey," Hattie said with a smile as Margo slipped off her coat.

Hattie turned back to the stove and lifted a spoonful out of the tall pot on the stovetop. She blew the steam away and tasted it gingerly with her lips. "Just right," she said, as she set the spoon aside.

Margo wandered over to the stove, drawn by the hearty smell of beef, and wrapped her arm around Hattie. She peered into the pot and inhaled appreciatively. "They're in for a treat. The perfect meal for a cold winter day."

Hattie squeezed her back. "And your sunny smile. What more could they need?"

Margo rested her head briefly on Hattie's shoulder. She needed this. More than they needed her, she needed them. "Bowls and spoons might be useful," she said as she pulled away. "What else can I do?"

"We have some rolls there. You could put them out. It's a hearty stew with carrots and peas, so no salad tonight. But a bit of bread might be good for sopping up the broth."

"Wonderful." Margo prepared the baskets of buns and then filled the sink to start the washing up.

"Ottie's best friend is out there again today," Hattie remarked.

Margo's heart skipped a beat. "Really?"

"Yessiree. Hasn't missed a day. Even with a sling on his arm, he's there givin' Ottie grief over the latest Shields loss."

Margo snorted. "Is he taking back the ice cream?"

"Oh, no. Ottie would never risk that. But that blond hair sure looks nice under that black top hat."

Margo rolled her eyes as she plunged her hands in the hot water and started on the dishes that Hattie had used to make the stew. "Seriously? He took the hat?"

Hattie shrugged and smiled. "Ottie'd sooner give up his hat than his ice cream." She transferred the stew to a serving dish and disappeared into the dining room.

Margo worked away at cleaning up the kitchen until Hattie poked her head in.

"Carl's here."

Margo nodded and dried her hands. She poured glasses of juice and water and carried them out to the dining room, opening the swinging door with her hip.

Carl was in his usual spot and looked and smelled a lot fresher than the week before.

"Things back to normal, Carl?"

"Yup, I'm back at the Y and back to work. I waited an extra two days, but the tests are clear. I let it run hot to be sure."

Margo nodded. If that's what it took to get him clean and productive, it was worth it. "I'm glad it worked out. They probably missed you at work."

Carl nodded. They chatted for a few more minutes and then Margo turned to head back to the kitchen.

It was odd to see Ottie's hat on someone else's head. Trace sat with his back to her, but she could see the sling around his neck. She hesitated, but her heart pulled her over.

Ottie laughed at something Trace said and looked up when she reached the table. "Hi, Doc. I hear you fixed up wonder boy here."

Trace turned laughing eyes to Margo. Her heart melted.

"I might not have, if I thought he'd take your hat," Margo said.

Ottie hooted. "Better watch your step," he said to Trace.

"Maybe you should help him with his gambling addiction," Trace said, trying to look innocent.

"Hard to when everyone is enjoying butterscotch ripple," Margo said.

Ottie laughed and slapped the table. "Don't you worry, he only gets the hat during dinner. It's going home with me."

"I don't know. It's a heckava lot warmer than I realized," Trace said. "I kind of like it."

"Don't get your hopes up. Shields are on a winning streak."

Trace and Ottie laughed, and Margo left them arguing about who was the better team.

Margo finished washing the last of the bowls when Trace strolled in. He handed her the dirty cutlery he carried.

Margo looked at him. "How's the shoulder?"

"Not bad. Occasionally hurts at night when I roll on it, but during the day, it's pretty good. I've been doing physio, and it feels more stable. Should be able to get the sling off in a week."

Margo raised her eyebrows. "That's fast. Excellent."

He nodded. "Everyone tells me how lucky I was to get it reduced right away. Made the difference they say."

Margo dried her hands and picked up a bowl from the rack. She nodded. "That's good. It was lucky."

"Lucky I was hanging out with a smart doctor."

Margo bit her lip. Lucky she didn't cause a bigger problem by reducing a dislocation that was actually a fracture.

With his good hand, Trace picked up the clean bowls as she dried them and stacked them neatly in the cabinet. "You got home okay on Saturday?" he asked.

"Oh yeah. It was quick. Did you hear how the rest of the weekend went?"

He nodded. "They said it was good. Conditions got a bit icy on Sunday, but no mishaps. Jess dropped your stuff off with mine. I need to get it back to you."

"I can swing by and pick it up. We started a new job this week, and I have to work late tomorrow night. Thursday I'll be back here. Maybe Friday?" Margo offered.

"Perfect," Trace agreed. "Come for dinner. We can reheat some of Mrs. Crombie's leftovers."

Margo's heart tattooed in her chest. She walked into that one. She shouldn't. She really shouldn't. "Ahh . . ." She turned away and racked her brain for a reasonable excuse.

Trace came up behind her. With his good hand, he brushed the hair away from the back of her neck and kissed the exposed skin. "Please."

Margo shivered from her head to her toes.

"Come see my new painting." He kissed her again.

Margo sighed. "I'd love to."

Chapter 22

Was it wrong to have sex with someone when you had no hope of having a long-term relationship? Margo rolled the pale gray paint onto the wall. She could understand going into sex, thinking he was the one, only to find out it was a disappointing mismatch. Socks on, ugly-colored bed sheets, intolerable wall color, clashing pheromones, those were all understandable deal breakers. You thought it would work, you tested the waters, but lo and behold, it wasn't meant to be. So you walk away. Fair enough.

But what if you knew right from the start that the long haul was only a dream?

There was no way she could ever meet Trace's family. She was too ashamed to admit what she'd done. And now, he had this trumped up image of her as a doctor that was completely false. She was up there on a pedestal all alone. It was never going to work.

She knew it. She could accept it. Eventually, she would accept it. She'd have to.

In the meantime, though, could she play out the dream?

Chloe walked into the room, carrying a takeout bag. "Time for a dinner break. I've got chocolate shakes and Thai turkey burgers with goat cheese."

"Bless you," Margo said as she set down the roller in the tray.

They sat on the floor with their backs against the wall, looking out over the city.

"This room has a spectacular view," Chloe said between bites. Lights below twinkled and the faint glow of the moon on the frozen lake reflected in the distance. "It'll be interesting to see what furniture they decide to put in here with this wall color. It's shaping up to be a swank hotel."

"Rivermede needed this. The water is drawing a lot more visitors. Winterfest is growing bigger, and the sailing regatta last summer pulled in a lot of people." Margo picked up her shake and waved it toward Chloe. "I personally like the idea of more B and Bs. Smaller, more intimate." Margo smiled. "But I won't complain about the pay check."

"Especially with the overtime," Chloe added.

"Exactly." Margo bit into the burger and groaned. "Delicious."

They sat eating their meal, watching traffic crawl along on the city street below. The odd person walked briskly down the street, huddled against the cold wind.

Margo's cell phone buzzed with a text message. She reached over and grabbed it from the pocket of her tote bag. Trace.

"Who is this one putting a sparkle in your eye?" Chloe asked.

Margo looked up to see Chloe eyeing her curiously. "Trace Bennett," she said slowly.

"Bennett? Of Bennett fame and fortune?"

"Unfortunately, yes."

"Unfortunately? Sounds like the perfect marriage. Construction and painting. Couldn't get any more convenient."

Margo winced. "I don't think Trace is into the family business."

"No?"

"No. He's finishing a master's degree in math. He's applying to medicine."

Chloe whistled. "A smart dude. Right up your alley."

Margo smiled weakly.

"Is he cute?"

"Very."

"Is he good in bed?"

"Chloe," Margo said, "that's personal."

Chloe nodded with a grin. "You haven't done the deed."

Margo tried to ignore her and took a sip of her milkshake.

"But you want to." Chloe nodded and finished up her burger. "What's he want?"

"I don't know if he wants to," Margo said. He did. She was pretty sure he did.

Chloe snorted. "All guys want to. I meant, why did he text you?"

"Oh." Margo looked at the text. "I have to drop by his condo tomorrow, and he invited me to dinner. He's confirming the time."

Chloe wiggled her eyebrows at Margo. "He's got it bad."

"What?"

"He's thinking about you. He's making sure you're thinking about him. He's got it bad."

"He's arranging the time. Maybe he has a lot of stuff he's juggling, and he's making sure he can fit me in."

"Oh, no. If he was fitting you in, he would have texted tomorrow. The day-before-text means he's anticipating. He's planning. You've found yourself a planner, girl. Their foreplay is extensive. You all waxed and ready?"

"Chloe." Margo winced. "I don't want to talk about it."

"Suit yourself." Chloe shrugged. "But I'd stack up on *extra* large condoms. Planners usually need 'em."

Chapter 23

Margo knocked on the door of Trace's condo and unbuttoned her coat. The longer dark brown wool coat was great for keeping her warm, especially when she wore a long sweater over leggings, but inside it quickly became too hot. She adjusted her purse, shifted the six-pack of beer to her other hand, and waited. A shadow flit across the peephole, and the door opened.

"You always use your peephole? Very commendable. You can never be too cautious," Margo teased.

Trace hid a smile. "Everyone has a dark side," he said, his blue eyes twinkling.

Margo's smile faded and she looked away. True. Too true.

She handed him the beer. "For you. I wasn't sure how hard it would be to carry beer home with your arm in a sling. So in case your supply is getting low."

"Thank you. Luckily my drinking arm is fine, and beer is always welcome."

Her snowboard, overnight case, and sleeping bag were sitting inside the door. "Oh, great. They didn't forget the sleeping bag," Margo said with a wry grin. She set her purse down and removed her coat.

Trace took it and threw it over the back of a chair. "I'd hang it up, but . . ." He pointed to his arm in the sling.

Margo laughed. "Good gig to get out of housework. She stopped and looked at the living room. "This looks really good." She turned three hundred and sixty degrees, her hands on her hips. A dark gray sofa in a soft chenille fabric faced the window, and a black reclining chair beside a metal floor lamp filled the corner. A modern piece of artwork, a stylized horse in full speed, almost flying, hung above the sofa. "Love what you've done with the place," she said with a fake British accent.

Trace grinned. "Good feng shui."

The walls looked good. The paint was smooth and the finish homogenous. The color was perfect with the black and gray furniture. It had a good vibe going.

She followed Trace into the kitchen. A thin black sweater strained across his chest. She wanted to run her hands down it. His jeans molded his thighs and butt. She just wanted.

She needed a drink.

"Would you like a beer or a glass of wine?" Trace asked.

Margo tried not to blush. *He couldn't read her mind, could he?* "Whatever you're having."

He pulled out two beers, popped the caps off, and handed her one. She took a gulp and coughed when she choked.

Trace rubbed her back. "You okay?"

No. No she wasn't. He was very close. He smelled like fresh laundry. His blue eyes were gorgeous. His hand was gentle, his smile genuine. Thankfully, his arm was in a sling.

"Fine," she managed. She stepped back.

"I'm heating up lasagna," Trace said. "Mrs. Crombie said to give it half an hour. She heard you were coming and brought over some homemade bread and her famous chocolate chunk cookies."

"She's the best."

"Let's sit in the living room. She told me to tell you that she loves helping out at Breaking Bread. I see her there every Monday and Wednesday."

"Hattie's thrilled with her, too." She sipped her beer. "Hattie also likes having you around."

"I caught on quick. Help Hattie with the dishes, and you're a friend for life."

Margo laughed. "Yes. That's absolutely true. But I think she also has a soft spot for Ottie. She likes that you sit with him, make him laugh, talk hockey with him. He really enjoys your company."

"Yeah, it's easy. He roots for the wrong team, but other than that, he's cool."

Margo laughed. "You're a bad influence with your gambling."

"He's worse," Trace said immediately. "He started it. Somebody should've warned me about him."

"And spoil all Ottie's fun? I don't think so. Plus everyone benefits with the butterscotch ripple."

Trace threw his head back and laughed. "I'm glad you suggested it. I enjoy it as much as Ottie does." He sipped his beer. "My application is almost done. We'll have to celebrate when I send it off."

She nodded. "It's a big job. Congrats." She looked out the window at the frozen lake below. It was a clear night and the moon was a bright crescent among the shimmering stars. "Have you thought about what you'll do if, you know, you don't get in?"

"Trying to break it to me gently that I don't have what it takes?"

Margo sat straighter. "No, not at all. I think you'll make an excellent doctor. You're outgoing, friendly, smart. You enjoy people. You treat everyone at Breaking Bread with respect. I really admire that. No. I'm not worried that you won't get in, but they always ask that question at the interviews."

Trace looked at her and didn't say anything. He leaned over and kissed her. "That means a lot. Thank you. As soon as this sling's off, I'll thank you properly." He sat back.

He started talking. Margo let out a breath slowly and tried to pay attention.

". . . PhD position or teacher's college. There are a few things I could do."

Margo nodded and sipped her beer. He was going to thank her properly. Just as soon as the sling was off. He was going to thank her properly. Frosty blues focused on her. His hands on her. His mouth, his tongue . . .

She took another sip of beer and set the bottle down with shaking hands. His words were more potent than the alcohol.

Chapter 24

Margo managed to get through the meal. She paid attention to what Trace said. Mostly. If she was distracted by his pale blue eyes, it was his own fault. Same for the broad chest and muscular thighs. They begged attention. She thought she'd done a pretty good job balancing all the distractions.

They made ice cream sandwiches with Mrs. Crombie's delicious chocolate chunk cookies, and Margo's heart melted with the ice cream.

She needed to come clean. Enough. She was tired of hiding the fact that she knew his grandfather, that she had been part of the medical team taking care of him when he died, that she was so very sorry about the care she provided. He needed to know. She took a deep breath and when the conversation slowed, decided it was right. She would lay it on the table and deal with the fallout.

Then his friends dropped by and invited them out for a drink.

And the moment was lost.

She was such a chicken.

Margo rolled paint on the wall and ruminated. She had worked late every night that week, trying to do the work of two people. Chloe had asked for the week off back in October, and since the end of January was traditionally a slow time for painting, she had agreed.

The job at the hotel was an unexpected bonus. It filled the gap until the job for Bennett homes started. Plus, outstanding student loans. The bank was always happy when she took on extra work.

Not having Chloe around made her appreciate her help that much more. The 6 a.m. starts and 10 p.m. finishes kept the schedule on track but were wearing thin. She arrived in the dark and left in the dark. She missed her shifts at Breaking Bread. She hadn't seen Trace.

He had sent her regular texts all week with a few more questions to finish off his application.

Today, she thought with surprise. It was due today. He'd be sending the whole package into cyberspace.

It was a scary feeling hitting that send button. No more revisions possible, and your future handed over for someone else to decide. She remembered that day. Probably because it came on the heels of a wild argument with her mother. Wild was probably exaggerating. It was more of a tense, clipped tone, unsmiling face, interaction. Her mother had made it pretty clear she wouldn't support her. Fine. She'd make it on her own. And she did. Financially, anyway. Emotionally, she could have used a hand.

She finished the last stroke on the wall and set the roller brush down. Done. Finally. She arched her back and brushed the hair away from her face.

The designer was hoping to move furniture in on the weekend, and the following week it was already booked. They didn't fool around. On Monday, they'd start the whole process again on the next floor.

She hammered the lid back on the paint can and gathered up the brushes to wash at home. Luckily the clean up was mindless, because she didn't have the energy to think.

Drop cloths folded, shoved in the tote bags. Tools packed in the pockets. Trays, rollers, and tape in the trash. Hot bath. Sleep. Can't wait.

The knock on the door startled her.

She walked over and opened it.

"You didn't check the peephole," Trace said with a shake of his finger.

Margo looked at him. She missed him. She wanted to take a step closer, wrap her arms around him, and lean her head on his shoulder. She wanted to feel his strong arms around her and inhale the fresh scent of his skin.

But she didn't move. "I'm a risk taker."

Trace grinned. "Good." He looked around the room. "Looks like I timed this perfectly. All done?"

She raised her eyebrows. "Just about. I have to carry this stuff up to the eighth floor so it's ready for Monday."

Trace picked up the totes and the can of paint. "Lead the way."

Margo picked up the rest of her stuff and headed out the door. "You just thought you'd drop by and help clean up?" She gave him a quizzical look.

"More or less," he said with a smile as they waited for the elevator.

"Can you carry that stuff? Where's your sling?"

"All better," he said with a smile. "Thanks to the quick action of a young, and beautiful, I might add, doctor. No sports for a few more weeks, but it's much better."

Margo smiled. "That's great." She fished out the key to the storage room and gestured for Trace to put the totes along the wall with the cans of paint, brushes, and rollers.

"Lot of stuff," Trace said.

Margo nodded. "It's a big job."

Trace looked at her. "You look tired."

"It's been a long week. TGIF." She locked the storage and stood awkwardly in the hallway. She wasn't sure how many streaks of paint were on her face or in her hair. She hadn't eaten since an early lunch, and the shower she'd had that morning seemed a long way off. "Thanks for the help," she said, still a little puzzled.

"You're welcome," Trace said. He kissed her lips softly. "Will you come with me?"

Margo's eyes fluttered open. She tilted her head at him and then nodded.

Trace smiled and grabbed her hand. He led her back to the elevator and they rode to the top floor. They walked down a short hallway, past a narrow table with fresh flowers, their feet sinking into the plush carpet. At the last door, Trace pulled out a key card and swiped the keypad. The door unlocked.

Margo looked at him, but he held the door open and waved her inside.

Soft music filled the air and flames flickered in a gas fireplace. A table was set for two with fine white linens and sparkling silver. Across the room, the lights from the city splashed a colorful background against the night sky. She took a trembling breath and inhaled the sweet scent of roses. The bed, in a private alcove, piled high with cushions, its fluffy duvet pulled back invitingly, was covered in rose petals.

Margo stood, taking it all in, her heart pounding.

Trace turned her to face him. He wrapped his arms around her and placed his forehead against hers. "I want to give you a special evening. I know you brush it off, but I couldn't have done what I did in the past four weeks without you. I sent the application off today, and I want to celebrate. With you." He pressed his lips to hers and teased her lips apart. His tongue danced inside and swept across her lips.

Margo felt her heart trip. As he tasted and teased, a lovely warmth swirled in her chest, and she pressed against him. She ran her hands up his arms and felt the muscles bunch beneath her hands.

Trace nipped at her lower lip when she groaned. He pulled back slowly, and she stared into his intense blue eyes.

"They'll bring dinner up in about an hour. Would you like to unwind in the hot tub?"

"Where have you been all my life?"

Trace chuckled. "This isn't how you usually spend Friday night?"

He lifted her shirt over her head and tossed it aside. He held her hands and trailed soft kisses across the lacy edge of her bra. Her breasts swelled as his tongue dipped under the fabric. Margo caught her breath at the light touch. She ached for more.

Trace reached behind and unclasped her bra. As he drew it away, his eyes darkened. Margo reached for him, but he held her shoulders and turned her around. "Look."

She looked at the reflection in the window as he pressed her back against him and ran his hands across the soft mounds of her breasts. Her breasts felt heavy and her nipples hardened against his palms. He kneaded and stroked with his thumbs, trailing soft kisses along her neck. Margo watched as he ran his hands down her belly and slowly stroked back up. Her legs turned to liquid. She leaned her head against him and reached back to hold him. She needed to touch him, but he held her tight. He followed the curve of her hip with his touch, spanning her waist, undoing the clasp on her jeans.

Margo watched their reflection. Her naked. Him behind her. His hands on her breasts. She caught his eye and swallowed. There was too much light and possibly too much scrutiny.

He stopped her from turning. "Uh-uh. You're beautiful," he whispered.

His fingers traced a line across her hips and coaxing her legs apart, took their time exploring the softness. He strummed and stroked, his fingers dancing across her wet flesh. Sensation slowly swirled and Margo whimpered. She twisted and arched, her heart racing and her breath catching. She tried to stop the whirlwind from building. Her arms, too heavy to raise, reached behind and clung to him. She glanced at the reflection in the glass.

Sleepy eyes, flushed cheeks, the wanting, the building, the pressure. Don't stop. Don't stop. Tremors racked her body and Trace held her tight, until her muscles went limp.

Margo felt like she was floating and never wanted to touch the ground. Trace kissed her temple and took her hand. He led her to the hot tub, filled with steaming water, and held her hand as she stepped in. As she sank down to her chin, he flipped a switch and silent bubbles filled the tub.

Trace lit the candles scattered around the room. The sweet scent of the roses, pink, pale orange, and delicate yellow, filled the air. Margo inhaled deeply.

Trace stood in front of her and pulled his shirt over his head.

"Mmmm . . ." Margo hummed in her throat.

He unfastened his jeans and pulled them down.

Margo's eyes widened. Chloe was right. She needed the extra-large.

He slipped in beside her, water sloshing over the side of the tub.

She curled against him, her soft breast against his hard chest, her hands very happy. His skin was smooth, his chest broad. The muscles of his six-pack rippled as she swept across. Lower still and down his long lean length. Bulging thighs. She stroked back up. A soft and silky wrapper with a hard throbbing core.

Trace crushed his lips to hers and sensation exploded in her head. Water sloshed to the rhythm of the quick stroking of her hand.

Trace groaned and bucked, and she stilled. He kissed her deeply once more before leaning back, his breathing ragged, and his body relaxed.

Margo cuddled close. Trace wrapped his arm around her and gently caressed her back under the water. Bubbles permeated up around them, and Margo listened to the beating of Trace's heart against the jazz music playing in the background.

"This is magical." She smiled. "You're a mathemagician," she whispered, placing a kiss on his lower jaw.

"And you're an artist with your hands," he said back, kissing the top of her head.

Margo smiled and wiggled closer.

Trace's body responded.

"He's an active one," she said with a laugh, running her hand across his belly.

"So much to see, so many places to explore."

When the bath water cooled, Trace helped Margo out of the tub and wrapped her in the fluffy white bath towel.

When she started to dry off, he stopped her. "Let me," he said. He unwound the towel, and as if handling fine china, dried her skin. She stood before him, conscious of his gaze. He picked up scented lotion and massaged it into her shoulders. Margo closed her eyes and sighed at his touch. Light fresh lime and citrus infused her skin as he circled around her breasts. He paused with his hands and laved her nipples with his tongue. She strained against his touch and grabbed his shoulders as he stroked and nipped across her belly, down her thighs, behind her knees and onto her calves. She tingled and shivered.

"I need to touch you," she said.

"I want that, too. But not yet."

At a knock on the door, Trace grabbed the robes, hanging on hooks. He helped Margo with hers and belted his tight. "Are you hungry?"

Margo looked at him. "Yes. But not for food."

Trace chuckled and went to open the door. He took the two bags of food from the deliveryman, tipped him, and shut the door. He turned to Margo. "Dinner. I ordered seafood risotto with lobster and scallops, an avocado and lime salad, and chocolate mousse with raspberries for dessert." He raised a brow at her. "We can eat it hot now or cold later."

Margo's stomach grumbled.

"Just one thing." He walked toward her, a bag in each hand, until he stood in front of her. "It tastes better if you're naked," he said with a smile, challenging her.

"Really?"

"Absolutely."

"I've always wanted to eat lobster risotto on a bed of roses," she said.

"Really?"

"Absolutely."

"Then I guess it's your lucky day," he said.

Margo untied her robe and pushed it from her shoulders, so it landed at her feet. She picked up the cutlery and linen napkins from the table and looked over her shoulder. "Coming?"

Chapter 25

Margo sat on an overturned bucket and checked her phone. The job at the hotel hadn't slowed any in the past two weeks, despite Chloe returning to work. They were stalled for the moment until the primer in the current suite dried.

Her phone had become her link to Trace. They had texted back and forth, and she followed him on Twitter and Facebook. Crappy way of dating, but with her crazy hours, she didn't have much choice. With his daily tweets, at least she felt like she knew what was going on in his life. One hundred and forty characters at a time.

The pace of her job wouldn't last. She knew it. Didn't make it any easier when she was in the midst of it, though. Another week, max, and the hours would get better. When it slowed, she had plans. Skin-to-skin contact, face-to-face time, and a two-way conversation more than one hundred and forty characters long.

She scrolled until she found his tweet.

The kids are bored. Send toys. Ricky wants sticker books. Adrian wants Lego.
#givewhatyoucan #KidsCancerCenterwaitingroom

Margo smiled. He had started a job attached to a research project at the Children's Cancer Center. When he jumped in, he really jumped in.

"Another tweet from your boyfriend?" Chloe teased. She sat cross-legged on the floor and popped a banana mini-muffin in her mouth.

Margo looked over and grinned. "He's campaigning for

waiting room toys for the Children's Cancer Center."

"Good cause. He must like kids, eh? That would explain why he was at the sperm donor clinic two weeks ago."

Margo's eyes widened and she twisted, almost falling off the bucket. "What?"

Chloe took a sip of her mango juice and swallowed. "Yeah. I saw him there. I need sperm, obviously, as part of my baby bump mission. So I thought I'd check out the withdrawals offered at the sperm bank. They're very stingy with their information, actually." She waved a piece of muffin in the air. "How does one choose between 4859 and 4562? They're numbers," she said with a frown.

"They probably vet them carefully and match the characteristics you request."

"That's true. But what if there's a reverse trait?"

"A reverse trait?"

"Yes, one that would throw up a stop sign. Make me want to reverse the process and rewind the clock. I have to live with the sperm-spawn for the rest of my life. I don't want to risk a reverse trait."

"Ah . . . I see your point."

Chloe smiled broadly. "So I applied for a job at the clinic."

Margo started. "What?"

Chloe nodded, a smug smile on her face. "Even got an interview. It went pretty well, I thought."

"You're kidding."

"No. I did really well."

Margo shook her head. "No, I meant, you didn't really apply for another job?"

"Sure did. But don't worry. It's only weekends nine to three. Receptionist. Full meet-and-greet duties, general dogsbody, and the biggest bonus, full access to all the files."

"Chloe," said Margo. "That information is supposed to be confidential."

"I won't tell anyone."

Margo shook her head.

Chloe popped the last of her mini-muffin in her mouth. "Once I choose the perfect sperm and have a baby swimming inside me, I'll quit. Simple. Anyhow the interview was two weeks ago and lo and behold, who should walk in? Trace Bennett."

"Really? Are you sure it was Trace?"

"Tall, blond, built, with incredible blue eyes?"

Margo frowned. He would do that? Donate sperm and be the anonymous father of a child? Granted, it was very altruistic. And didn't she coach him about just that? Encourage him to take on projects to advocate for health and well-being? Yes, yes she did. And after all, it was his sperm. But still, she had a stake in that sperm now. Sort of. She sighed. Not really.

"I am definitely interested in a squirt from that vessel. I think we would make beautiful babies," Chloe said with a mischievous grin.

Margo looked at her with wide eyes and felt her stomach burn. No. No. That was so not right. "B-B-But . . ." Before she could speak, her phone beeped with a text message. From Trace.

Hey, Breaking Bread tomorrow?

She had already missed two weeks. It was enough. The painting was close enough to the deadline that she could afford an evening for herself.

Yes. I can go. I'll see you there?

She smiled at her phone, shut it off, and dropped it in the tote. "Let's get this job finished, Chloe. I'm tired of watching paint dry."

Chapter 26

Margo stepped out of her car, trying to avoid the icy patch covering most of the Breaking Bread parking lot. She missed the sunny skies of January. The first eleven days of February had been gray and dull, and the piles of snow plowed off the parking lot were taller than her Mini-Cooper.

"Hello, beautiful."

Margo turned and smiled. Trace. He swept her close and covered her mouth with his. Margo pressed closer, her lips eager against his.

She lightly stroked the cool skin of his cheek. "Hi, handsome."

Trace smiled and crushed his lips to hers, inviting her tongue to join him. Sensation built. Her breasts felt heavy, the swirl in her belly a lovely pull.

She sighed and pulled back slowly. "We should go in."

Trace brushed his lips against hers. "We should." He slipped his gloved hand in her open jacket and ran his hand down the curve of her breast. "Maybe after, we could find someplace warmer." He ran his tongue along her jaw. "And more private."

Margo's skin tingled, and she shivered.

"Because I miss the feel of your skin," Trace whispered in her ear.

Visions of their evening together swam in her head. Margo fleetingly contemplated getting back in her car, pretending she never arrived, and taking Trace with her. "You're a bad influence," she said, reluctantly stepping back.

Trace grinned. "What?" he asked innocently.

She shook her head and grabbed his hand, tugging him toward the door. "Work first," she said, turning her head to smile at him. "Then play."

Later, cuddled naked beside him, feeling satisfied and sleepy, she ran her fingers across his skin.

Trace had pulled light sheers across the wall of windows in his bedroom, but she could see the hazy light of the moon. The lake was still frozen, and the reflection of the moonlight on the snow, covering the wide expanse of the ice, brightened the sky.

"Would you be able to get off early on Thursday?"

Margo smiled. "For more of this?"

"Absolutely," he said with a grin. "It's Valentine's Day. You'll be my Valentine, won't you?"

"Absolutely," she said with a smile.

"I have plans. But I'd have to pick you up at three-thirty," he said.

"Oh. Plans, eh? Sounds intriguing. Am I privy to your plans?"

He shifted and pushed her gently onto her back. He ran his hand across her breasts and teased the sensitive skin. "There'll be some of this." He trailed kisses across her jaw. "And some of that." He continued down the ticklish side of her neck toward the soft skin of her breast. "Definitely some of this." His tongue swept across her nipple. He tasted and teased and nipped with his teeth.

Margo arched toward him and groaned. "Thursday's shaping up to be my favorite day of the week."

Trace chuckled and continued the slow exploration of her skin with his lips and tongue. Across her belly and lower still, until Margo was writhing and bucking and grabbing his hips to guide him in.

Lying sweaty and spent, Margo turned to look at Trace. "Three-thirty you said? I'll be ready."

Trace removed the condom. He interlaced his fingers with hers, and after a few minutes, threw a blanket over the two of them.

"I should go," Margo said in a sleepy voice, not making a move to leave. "I have to be up at six tomorrow morning."

"Stay," Trace said, brushing her curls away from her face. "I have to be at the hospital at eight, so we can get up together."

"Really?"

Trace smiled and kissed her deeply.

Margo snuggled closer and let her hand wander. She loved the feel of his skin over the hard muscles of his abdomen. Across his thighs, feeling the muscles bunch. Dancing lightly over the warm skin. "How's your new job going?"

Trace lifted her hand and kissed it. When he released it, she continued a trail across his skin.

"It's good. I'm almost finished collecting the data. They thought they were done, but in order to run the stats, I needed some baseline information. So I'm interviewing some of the kids and parents again."

"These are all kids with cancer?"

"Yeah. And they've had at least one round of chemotherapy."

Margo sighed. "That's rough."

Trace was silent. She could feel the muscles of his belly ripple as she stroked his side.

"Some of those kids are tough," Trace said finally. "They've been through a lot of shit. At that age, I was playing hockey after school, learning how to snowboard, running around at our cottage in the summer–"

"Being a kid."

"Yeah, being a kid. They don't get to be kids. May never get to be adults either." Trace sighed.

Margo turned her cheek and kissed his chest. "I saw your tweet asking for toys. You're helping them be kids."

"In a small, small way. But, yeah. The response has been amazing. Some pretty awesome stuff has been sent in."

She heard the sadness in his voice. "Part of medicine is helping patients get through the hard stuff. We can't always take away the suffering," she said as she kissed him softly again. "But you didn't ignore it, either. You saw a way to brighten their day in the midst of all the black. And that's a good thing."

Her hand stroked and his body stirred. She wanted him inside. She wanted to soothe away the sorrow.

She trailed kisses across his chest as she shifted and straddled his waist. His hands came up to touch her skin. Not soothing, not softly, but yearning with need. He reared his head and caught her breast. Margo arched as he sucked and nipped, driving her higher. His hand slipped lower and found her wet and full and ready.

Margo ripped open a condom and batted his hand aside. She wanted him. She needed him now. She slid the condom on, loving the feel as he throbbed, and guided him inside. Gently first, then tightening around him. Moving and rocking, sliding and pressing. He grabbed her hips and thrust deeper. Margo's breath caught. A sheen of sweat covered her skin. Sensation built and caught in her throat as she rose up and finally contracted around him. Trace, fast behind her, pumped his release.

Margo collapsed on his chest, her muscles languid as the tremors subsided, and listened to the rapid beat of his heart. Trace wrapped his arms around her and held her tight.

"I don't think I can move," Margo murmured. "I haven't felt this relaxed . . . since I saw you last."

Trace chuckled. "You're welcome." He loosened his hold and rolled her over onto her back. "That was just the main course. We still have dessert."

Margo smiled. "And I do have a sweet tooth."

He trailed kisses across her collarbone. "I love the taste of your skin."

Margo sighed as he nibbled and kissed. "Trace?"

"Hmmm . . ."

"Would you ever donate to a sperm bank?"

Trace sat back and looked at her. "I've thought about it. I read an article about a woman who had trouble conceiving. How grateful they were to have access to a sperm bank." He shrugged. "I thought it was something I could do. Why?"

"I just wondered." Margo looked away.

"Do you think it's a good thing? Or bad?"

Margo frowned and tried to turn away. But he held her shoulder. "I think there are a lot of women who would welcome your sperm," she said finally.

Trace grinned.

"I just don't like the thought of sharing. I know, truly, it's none of my business. But I'm a one-person-sperm-recipient at a time, kinda girl."

Trace kissed her lips. "I'm a one-person-sperm-giver at a time, too. I decided not to do it in the end."

"Really?"

"Yeah, really. All my sperm are yours, babe."

"Thanks," she said gratefully.

"But you're using birth control, right?"

"Oh God, yeah," she said with grin.

Chapter 27

Margo pulled a warm sweater over her head as the doorbell rang. She ran her hands through her curls trying to tame the worst of it and went to open the door.

Trace stepped in and pulled her close, crushing his lips to hers. She pushed aside his ski jacket and ran her hands under the soft cotton jersey he wore. Skin. Beautiful skin.

Why had he stressed that she should dress for the outdoors? There were too many layers. She was ready to start peeling them off.

Trace stepped back after one more short kiss. "Happy Valentine's Day," he said, his blue eyes twinkling.

"Happy Valentine's Day to you, too."

"Ready to go?"

Margo raised her eyebrows. "Where are we going?" She didn't really expect an answer. They had been playing this game for the last three days.

"It's a surprise," he said, his standard answer.

She gathered her hat and gloves and wound a scarf around her neck. "Okay, all set."

"Bring your snow pants, too," he said.

Margo shrugged and tossed her snow pants over her arm as she locked the door to her apartment. "I guess I'll finally get to see what kind of car you drive," she said smugly.

He smiled back, followed her outside, and steered her toward a sleek black limousine.

"Courtesy of Bennett Homes," he said as the driver opened the door for her.

Margo laughed as they climbed in together and settled

back. Champagne was chilling, and a mini-plate of cheese and crackers and chocolate-covered strawberries sat on a tray in front of them.

"Nice car," she commented as Trace fed her a strawberry.

"It's a special occasion. We have a half-hour ride, and I thought I'd enjoy the champagne with you."

"Good thinking," she said as she clinked her glass with his. "To Valentine's Day surprises that start with champagne and chocolate. It's already perfect." She leaned over and kissed him softly, tasting the champagne that lingered on his lips.

They sat back and enjoyed the smooth ride. The sun was getting low in the sky, but was still bright enough to glint off the snow covering the ground. They drove north into the countryside until solitary farmhouses were separated by acres of land.

They turned down a country lane and Margo caught a glimpse of a hot air balloon. "Oh. Look at the colors of that balloon. Gorgeous. Blue, green, orange, red. Look at the way the sun hits it. It's almost glowing. Wow," she said with a sigh. "I bet there'd be a spectacular view from a balloon."

Trace smiled. "I guess we'll find out."

"Really?" Margo said, grinning from ear to ear. "Really? I would die to go up in a hot air balloon."

The limo came to a stop.

"You are so getting lucky tonight," Margo whispered to Trace as she stepped out.

Trace chuckled and squeezed her hand. "I'm already lucky," he whispered back.

Trace walked, Margo skipped, hand in hand over to the balloon tethered in a field and introduced themselves to the pilot. Sean, a quiet man in his mid-forties, smiled broadly at Margo's enthusiasm and indicated they could climb inside the basket. He made a few adjustments to the ropes outside, tested his walkie-talkie, and then climbed in with them. As he opened the burner, he motioned for the two grounds crew to release the tether lines.

With a whoosh and a roar, the balloon filled and rose above the treetops. Margo gripped the edge and watched, fascinated, as the balloon caught the wind and soared silently across the field. Cool air brushed her cheeks. With Trace's arm around her, she was warm.

The occasional roar of the propane burner broke the silence as they glided along. Snow on the fields, tall evergreens, an array of bare deciduous trees, their branches like art in the sky, Margo drank it all in. The air was fresh with the occasional whiff of pine as they skimmed the treetops.

The pilot explained that the course they took varied with the wind, but a crew on the ground followed their path and would meet them with a truck where they landed.

Margo wished it would never end.

The sky lit up in layers of color. A wide band of pink changed to bright orange and mixed with burnt yellow as the sun set behind them.

After an hour, the pilot aimed for a field in the distance to bring them down. The ground rushed closer as the balloon lowered and finally touched down with a bump.

"Perfect." Margo leaned into Trace. "That was perfect."

The pilot secured the basket and the grounds crew rushed over and anchored the tether lines. Trace and Margo hopped out of the basket and were handed glasses of champagne.

"To a safe and successful ride," Sean said, raising his glass.

They clinked glasses and drank. Margo caught Trace's eye. "Thank you. I loved that," she said.

The limousine pulled up to where the balloon sat, slowly deflating.

"Thanks very much," Trace said as they shook hands with the pilot and crew. "We may be back for more."

The pilot grinned. "Hard to stay away once the bug catches you."

They waved good-bye and climbed into the limo.

Margo sighed. "It's going to be hard to top that."

"A challenge?" Trace asked with a grin.

She looked into his blue eyes and let her gaze travel over the square jaw, the broad shoulders. Remembering what was underneath all the layers, and what his hands and tongue and lips were capable of, she said, "You're right. It can only get better."

Chapter 28

The following Tuesday, Margo was up to her elbows in hot dishwater, still re-living the Valentine's Day evening. The balloon ride had only been the beginning. It had been followed by a limo ride to a cozy restaurant in the country for a five-star, four-course meal in a casual setting.

A wood-burning fire had crackled in the fireplace, soft music had filled the air, and the muted conversations of the other patrons in the small dining room had made it intimate and elegant.

They had ended up at Trace's condo with more soft music, dancing by the moonlight streaming in the windows, and a dreamy evening in bed.

He was thorough. He could definitely write that on his resume. Great with his hands, excellent skills with his tongue. She tingled thinking about it and told herself to stop. She was in the middle of a shift at Breaking Bread, and Hattie would be calling her out for daydreaming if she didn't start paying attention.

Trace was out in the dining room, doing his usual sparring with Ottie over hockey. She heard the occasional burst of laughter from the dining room when someone swung through the door to replenish the food or carry in the dishes.

First work. Then play. She looked around at the dwindling pile of dishes left to wash. It wouldn't be long.

The kitchen door swung open and Trace poked his head in. "Margo, can you come, please? Ottie's having chest pain."

Margo grabbed a tea towel and dried her hands as she hurried to the dining room. A small crowd of people hovered around Ottie, who sat in his usual chair. They parted to let Margo through.

Margo knelt down beside him. "Chest pain, Ottie?"

Ottie grimaced and nodded. "Here." He held his fist against the center of his chest. "And here." He motioned up his neck and down his left arm.

Trace stood beside him, frowning. He lifted Ottie's hat off. Ottie's face was pale, sweat gathered on his forehead, and he struggled to speak.

Margo looked up at Trace. "Call an ambulance."

Ottie looked even more distressed and became agitated. "No. I don't want that," he said.

Hattie clucked around. "Let's give him some room, everyone. Take a seat and give him some space."

Margo placed her fingers at Ottie's wrist and checked his pulse. "It could be your heart, Ottie. Have you had heart problems?"

"Years ago. Not recently."

Trace stepped back to the circle around Ottie. "They're on their way. Is there anything else I can do?"

Margo watched Ottie relax as Trace drew close. "Stay close by."

Trace knelt down beside Ottie. "Don't think I'm going to forget about our bet. This doesn't change anything."

Ottie gave a weak laugh and reached for Trace's hand.

The paramedics arrived within minutes and whisked Ottie onto a stretcher and into the waiting ambulance. He looked so small and frail, his little round face peaking out from under the blankets.

"We should go with him," Trace said with a worried glance. He picked up Ottie's top hat and brushed it off. "I wouldn't want to be on my own at the hospital, and he seems scared."

Margo watched the ambulance pull away. Her stomach burned with acid. Memories of Trace's grandfather filled her head. "Yeah. Yeah. We probably should."

Hattie hovered. "You go, honey. I'll finish the washing up. Everyone will feel better if they know you're with Ottie."

Margo smiled weakly. "Okay. I'll get my keys."

Trace followed on her heels.

Margo's mind was reeling. Back to the hospital. She vowed never to go back. It was going to be okay. She wasn't the doctor. She was just the friend of the patient. The moral support. She would watch what came out of her mouth. Think twice, speak once. Be very careful.

Ottie had chest pain, and it didn't look good. It sounded like angina. Could be a heart attack. It was possible he'd need a stent. What if she said the wrong thing again? She shouldn't reassure him. She shouldn't not reassure him. He was so anxious, poor thing. What if she messed up? What if it was Ernie all over again?

Margo felt the burn in her chest and wished she had an antacid in her car. Her pulse raced and her palms were sweating despite the cold air blasting through the vents.

They pulled up to the emergency department, and Margo slowed the car. She looked over at Trace. He was as pale as Ottie. His brows were together in a deep frown. He stared silently out the window and rubbed the brim of Ottie's hat.

"I'll drop you off at the door and park the car. Go find him and sit with him," she encouraged.

Trace nodded and stepped out. He strode through the emergency department entrance, his shoulders squared. *He'll be there for Ottie.*

She parked the car and made her way inside. Slowly. Any slower and she'd be walking backward, she chided herself. She looked around the room and didn't see Trace. She checked with the nurse and learned that Ottie was in a room and was only allowed one visitor.

She took a seat in the waiting room and picked up a magazine but couldn't focus on the stories. The words blurred on the page.

It was taking too long.

Margo was about to get up and pace when the door opened, and Trace walked through. He looked around and made a beeline for her. She stood up and walked into his hug.

"He's stable," Trace said. "It was touch and go for a while, but he's stable." He sighed as he held her. "It's his heart, and they want to put a stent in. I don't get all of what they were saying, but the gist is they want to put a little tube to hold the clogged artery open?"

Margo nodded. "Yes, that's right. When are they doing it?"

"They're waiting for a doctor, and as soon as he gets here, they're going ahead." He squeezed her and stepped back to look in her eyes. "Can you talk to him? He has a million questions, and I don't know the answers. You could explain it to him."

Margo's gut clenched and she felt lightheaded. "I . . . I can't."

Trace frowned. "Why not? I can wait out here if you're worried about the one visitor rule."

"I don't know what to say."

Trace snorted. "You gave me a dozen scenarios easier than this and knew exactly what to say."

"That was different."

"How? You're great with stuff like this."

Margo cringed. "I had time to think about those. I can't do it on the fly," she said, her voice rising with panic.

"That's ridiculous. Just do the same thing." He tugged her hand and pulled her toward Ottie's room.

Margo dug her heels in. She started to see black. Her head was floating away from her body. "I can't," she whispered. She blinked back tears.

"Margo, he needs you. He's scared. He has a million questions, and you can help him."

Margo stood still, her eyes filling. "I can't," she repeated.

Trace gave an impatient shake of his head. "What do you mean, you can't? You're a doctor. Of course you can." Trace sighed. "What are you going to do when you have patients who need you? Don't think of Ottie as a friend. Think of him as a patient."

Margo shook her head, her lips pressed together. She swallowed. "I'm never going to have patients. I'm a painter."

Trace snorted. "Right." He waved his hands impatiently. "Of course you'll go back to medicine. How can you not? Even Daniel thought you'd return."

Margo gritted her teeth. "It's not a passing thing. I'm not going back."

Trace stared. "You're going to throw it all away?" he asked, incredulous. "People apply for years, spend thousands of dollars to be a doctor. You have it in the palm of your hand, and you're going to throw it all away?"

Margo bit her lip and focused over his shoulder.

"That's a waste. And this is a cop out. Ottie really needs you." Trace threw her a scathing look and turned on his heel. He pushed through the door to the patient exam area and didn't look back.

Margo sat down heavily on a waiting-room chair and bowed her head in her hands. She couldn't be here.

She rose on shaking legs and walked out into the cold air.

Chapter 29

Ottie did okay. Margo's classmate was rotating through the cardiology service, so she called her each day for an update.

Three of his cardiac arteries had been blocked, and he had needed a stent. He had sailed through it with flying colors but stayed in the hospital for an extra few days because he lived alone. Now he was up and about and ready to go home.

She wasn't doing okay.

She hadn't heard from Trace.

She had stalked his Facebook page until yesterday, when he had unfriended her.

She followed him on Twitter, but his posts had become sparse. Except for one tweet the night before.

He got an interview. Only one, he tweeted.

But one was all you needed. Well, good luck to him. He was still keen. Probably cuz he hadn't killed anyone lately. His foray into the medical world with Ottie apparently hadn't turned him off medicine. Just her.

He was definitely turned off her. Unfriended. Disliked. Disdained. She was persona non grata. Whatever the hell that meant.

She glared at the lime green Volkswagen Beetle in front of her. Why would anyone want to drive a happy car all the time? People weren't happy all the time. And that color looked like spring. It was the middle of the freakin' freezing winter. The car needed a giant scarf.

She turned into the parking lot at Breaking Bread, and

her car slid two feet when she tried to stop. Time for some salt and sand.

Hattie was at the stove when Margo went in.

"Welcome, honey. Come in and get warm," Hattie shouted with a smile.

Margo breathed in the scent of spicy chili and baking bread. "Smells delicious, as usual," she said as she wrapped an arm around Hattie's shoulders.

Hattie squeezed her back. "Thank you. I made a big batch so we can freeze some. Maybe save us some cookin' and cleanin' one day next week."

"You always say that Hattie, but there are never any leftovers."

Hattie laughed and looked at Margo closely. Margo fidgeted with the scrutiny.

"What's with those dark circles? Where's your ready smile?"

"Rough week," Margo said, hoping to brush it off.

Hattie looked serious. "Yeah, I hear ya. Ottie sure gave us a scare last week, didn't he? But I hear he's doin' all right."

Margo nodded and tried to smile. "He is. He's pestering them to go home. But he did score some butterscotch ripple. I think he's charmed the nurses."

Hattie gave a deep laugh. "Sure, or maybe it was that boyfriend of yours. I hear he's been staying with Ottie, visiting him twice a day, making sure he's got a TV so he can watch the games. Keeping a real close eye on him." She stirred the chili. "And Trace would charm the butterscotch ripple out of the kitchen."

"He would."

"Never mind that. I'm still thanking the heavens that it happened on a night you were here. You knew what to do. Organizing it all, going with Ottie to the hospital, that meant a lot. He was pretty scared and a familiar face is always reassuring. We're lucky to have a doctor so handy," she said with a laugh.

Margo rubbed absently at the ache in her stomach. She was a fraud and a coward. "I think Trace did more."

Hattie nodded. "He's a fine boy, too. He dropped by and said he would take meals over to Ottie until Ottie was well enough to traipse through the snow. Isn't that the nicest thing?"

"Yeah. Really nice."

"That's what I thought, too. I hear he's going for a doctor. He'll make a good one. Too bad we're not the ones choosin'. I'd choose him for sure."

Better him than her. "I'll start with the washing up here, Hattie," she said, trying to change the subject.

"Perfect. This is all done. We'll get it served up." Hattie moved about the kitchen finishing the final touches, taking warm rolls from the oven, and supervising the buffet table for the meal.

Margo filled the sink and gathered the dishes, staying out of Hattie's way. She ventured out into the dining room to help Carl with his meds, but the atmosphere in the dining room wasn't the same without Ottie's cheerful grin and Trace's interested eyes.

Her heart was heavy as she shut the lights off at the end of the evening and locked the door behind her.

Margo shivered in the cold and pulled up her hood. This was fumble-with-the-key, no-way-are-the-gloves-coming-off, weather. Even the engine gave a low whine of protest in the cold when she inserted the key fob and pushed the button, but it caught and started. Rubbing her hands together to keep them warm, she sat for a moment to let the engine run.

She needed a holiday and really wanted to get away. Someplace tropical. Away from winter. Away from scrutiny and lies. Away from Trace. She sighed. Just away. She missed Mikaela and wondered what she was up to. Did ob-gyn residents get holidays?

She switched on the fan and blasted warm air onto the windshield to melt the frost on the inside and loosen the ice on the outside. It'd be another minute before she could go scrape it off, so she pulled out her phone.

Hey you up for a holiday? Desperate need for some vitamin D here.

She hit send. She grabbed the ice scraper and went out and cleared off the windshield. In the time it took, Mikaela answered.

Sounds wonderful. Maybe next week? On call next 2 days then off for 3. I'll try to finagle 2 more. Where?

Margo smiled and texted back. *Any place with palm trees.*

I'll get Nancy on it.

Bless Nancy's heart, Margo thought, as she set her phone aside. She turned her headlights on and pulled out of the parking lot. Home. She craved a long soak in the tub and a quiet night reading under the warmth of her comforter.

She sighed and felt the weight of weariness on her shoulders.

Margo pulled up behind a cube van at a red light. When the light turned green, the cube van shot off, and a huge chunk of ice slid off the roof and flew at Margo's Mini-Cooper.

It crashed down, bounced off the hood, and smashed into the passenger side windshield, shattering the glass into a thousand pieces.

Shit. Visions of a hot bath flew out the window as the cold air rushed in. What a hassle.

The cube van took off. Margo pulled over to the side of the road, hit the hazard light button with more force than it needed, and pulled out her cell phone.

She wasn't even sure who to call. She looked at the shattered windshield. A tow truck, for one. Police? Insurance?

Margo dealt with it all. Two hours later, she unlocked the door to her apartment and shuffled wearily inside. It was done. The car was at a garage. She'd have to call in the morning and sort out the details, but they estimated at least a week for the repair. The windshield was the easy part. It was the huge dent in the hood that was the problem. And the paint job that would have to follow the repair. And the money it would take to pay for the windshield and the paint job. And the insurance rates that would go up.

A week without a car. Great. She'd have to rent one.

More expense, but she'd need a car to earn money. Money she needed to pay for all the bills for the car.

She threw her keys on the table near the door, tugged off her boots, and shrugged out of her coat. Too tired to care, she tossed the coat on the nearest chair. She trudged to the kitchen and pulled out the bottle of wine she kept in the fridge for 'emergency' guests.

Damn. Where was a twist off top when you needed it? She scrounged through three drawers for a corkscrew. Not a bottle opener in sight.

Forget it.

She left the bottle on the counter and shutting off the lights, made her way to the bedroom. A bath. Hot water. Bubbles. A long soak. A long sleep.

Dreams of palm trees and warmth.

And a vacation she could afford.

Chapter 30

The good news was the insurance was going to cover the cost of the repair, minus the five hundred dollar deductible.

The bad news was they were going to take two weeks to do it.

The best news was that Nancy, travel agent extraordinaire, found a holiday in the Caribbean that fit Margo's meager budget.

Mikaela had managed to arrange time off, and one of the bodyguards from her father's company had been available to go with them. Being the daughter of a very public billionaire had its drawbacks. Traveling with a bodyguard in tow was one of them.

Two days into the holiday, Margo's stomach had finally stopped burning with pain. Her skin had gone from pasty white to faint brown, even with the judicious use of SPF 50.

Margo leaned back in the lounger floating in the pool and raised her face to the sun, soaking in the warmth. Coconut oil sunscreen had her smelling like the tropical drink she had ordered. It arrived with a little umbrella and fit neatly into the drink holder on the arm of the lounger. She dipped her toes in the warm water of the pool and lazily paddled closer to Mikaela.

"This was one of your better ideas," Mikaela said. Her shoulder-length brown hair was slicked back from a dip in the pool. Her bronze and turquoise bikini had dried as she floated on a matching lounger.

Margo heard a child's laughter and glanced over at a young family. They were splashing in the shallowest of the three spacious circular pools that separated the patio at the back of the hotel from a sandy beach. Stunningly artful placement of granite at one end of the pool created the backdrop for a babbling waterfall. Mikaela's bodyguard sat at a table close by, constantly scanning the horizon, but other than the young family and them, it was quiet.

"You think? Better than dying our hair purple for a school spirit day?"

Mikaela snorted. "That was a good idea, but lacked in the planning. It would have been handy to know that purple dye lasts approximately ten days."

"Excellent execution. Poor follow through."

"Made for interesting prom pictures," Mikaela said with a laugh and sipped her drink.

"We should probably grab some lunch and take a break from the mid-day sun," Margo suggested.

Mikaela nodded. "Yeah. Even in the shade, it's getting hot. What do you want to do this afternoon?"

"Rent motorcycles?" Margo said tongue-in-cheek.

They laughed together. "Ride an organ donor-cycle? There's an activity that's not going to happen," Mikaela said.

"I'm happy to sit on the beach under the shade of a hut and read. I want to shut my brain off, not make any decisions, and not worry."

Mikaela looked at her. "What are you worrying about?"

Margo leaned her head back. "What am I not worrying about?" She picked up her drink and twisted the umbrella. "The past, the present, the future."

"When do you have to make a decision about medicine?"

"I have to let them know by April third. They'll confirm by May second." She sipped her drink.

"Have you thought any more about what you're going to do?"

Margo smiled sadly. "Constantly, but not very constructively. I don't know what to do. I think I suck as a physician. I'm not happy doing it. And yet, I love it. I love listening to patients, trying to solve each mini-mystery they present with. But then I worry I suck at it and spend all my time ruminating. Did I say the right thing, make things worse instead of better?"

"You were a student," Mikaela protested.

"A clerk."

"A clerk is still a student. You're not expected to know what to say or do. Half the time, the supervisors are too busy to teach. You feel like you're always in the way, because you are. Let's face it, you don't really know enough to be helpful, and it's not worth their time to teach someone who's only rotating through and may never do that specialty again."

Margo took a drink to swallow the lump in her throat.

"If you love it, you should give it another chance. If you hated it, that would be a different story," Mikaela said gently.

"I hate the guilt."

"You shouldn't feel guilty."

"I told that patient he would live. And he died."

"You didn't kill him."

"I didn't expect him to die."

"No one did. The surgeon didn't. The anesthesiologist didn't. The patient had a bad disease. The team did what they could as fast as they could to save him, but nature had other plans."

"Nature sucks."

Mikaela smiled sympathetically. "Sometimes it does." She swirled her hand in the water. "Don't over think it."

Margo snorted. "Should add that to my mantra. First, do no harm. Second, don't over think it."

Mikaela shielded her eyes against the sun. "I ran into Daniel the other day."

Margo closed her eyes and leaned back. "How's he doing?" She hadn't spoken to him since the snowboarding trip.

"He looked tired, but it was the end of a twelve-hour day in surgery. He mentioned he's engaged."

Margo opened her eyes with a startled glance. "What?"

Mikaela shrugged. "Yeah. He had a goofy grin on his face when he talked about his fiancée. I think they plan on a spring wedding."

"They're not going to wait until he's done?"

"Apparently not. Although, I did hear a rumor that she might be pregnant."

"Really? After all those lectures about birth control? And a stint in the delivery suite?"

Mikaela laughed. "You'd think that would turn him off." She sobered. "I know you were sweet on him at one point, and I wasn't sure if you'd heard about the engagement."

"No, I hadn't. But it's okay. I've given my heart to someone else to break." She rested her head back against the chair and squinted in the sun, despite her sunglasses.

"Trace Bennett?" Mikaela asked.

"The one and only. I completely froze when one of the sweetest people you'll ever meet at Breaking Bread developed chest pain. I couldn't talk to him. All I thought about was Trace's grandfather and the effect of careless words. I didn't want to harm poor Ottie because he meant so much to me, and to Trace. So I walked away. Now Trace thinks I'm a selfish, two-faced bimbo who's carelessly throwing away a medical degree." She blinked back tears.

"He doesn't know you," Mikaela said, reaching over and squeezing her hand.

Margo looked off into the distance. "Maybe that is who I am."

"No." Mikaela shook her head emphatically. "It's not. You're a dedicated and compassionate doctor. You have too much heart, not too little. That was just shock. Made more difficult because you cared. Next time will be easier."

"If there is a next time." Margo gave a large sigh. "Painting is so much easier."

"There will be a next time. You wouldn't be content with easy for long."

A child's high-pitched squeal of laughter interrupted them. They looked over to watch the dad lift his daughter high in the air and swing her around. When he lowered her into the water, she splashed and kicked and raised her hands for more.

Mikaela looked over at the bar set in the edge of the pool. "Do you think they'd serve food to the middle of the pool?"

Margo looked over at the two bartenders, both male, both young. "Take your top off. That'll get us some service."

"Margo," said Mikaela, with a laugh. "That's terrible."

"What can I say? I do better with easy."

Chapter 31

Margo put her roller brush to the wall and thought about how much the blue-green color reminded her of the ocean. Which she had enjoyed for far too short a time.

She was back at work, last week's warmth and sunshine a distant memory. They had flown back on Saturday in Mikaela's father's private jet and touched down an hour before an ice storm hit. Most of the power in the city had been out all day Sunday, but by late evening, it had been restored.

Margo spoke briefly to Chloe and suggested she carry on with the work at the hotel. They were right on schedule, so Margo decided to squeeze in a residential job that she had promised to do a while back. It was a Bennett home she had painted the previous fall, but after living with builder's beige for a few months, the customer requested an upgrade. The room was spacious, but manageable, and this particular customer hadn't filled it with furniture or gone crazy with nail holes, so the preparation took no time at all.

She had started the day early and dropped by the car rental agency to pick up a car for the week. A little red Spark.

They had offered her a yellow hatchback. A. Yellow. Hatchback. Double whammy. She had visions of herself weaving down the road, changing lanes willy-nilly, and landing in a parking lot straddling two spots. Her appalled look had them scrambling for more paperwork. The Spark was a little smaller, a little cheaper to rent, and had snow tires. Much better.

She had crept along the ice-covered streets and kept a

safe distance from the car ahead of her. One ice accident was enough.

By early afternoon, clouds rolled in, and the gloomy skies out the window cast a gray tinge to the blue-green.

Margo picked up a brush to edge the top and bottom of the wall and thought about her choices.

Really, if she didn't go back and do a residency this year, she could forget about practicing medicine. She'd always have her medical degree. They couldn't take that away from her. But no residency, no license. Without a license, she couldn't practice. Was that how she wanted to leave it?

That was the million-dollar question.

What did she want?

She wiped a bit of blue-green paint off the baseboard and flicked on the overhead light. It was getting dark enough to need it.

She couldn't see herself not painting. The creativity, the variety, the satisfaction of a job well done, and the customer's reaction – she loved it all. Rolling paint on the wall was relaxing, and every time new color went on the wall, she imagined the possibilities, the inspiration from a fresh change. It was such a rush. She'd always need that.

But was it worthwhile? *Life is about using your skills to help others.* Her mother's voice echoed in her head.

Color made people feel better. It was worthwhile.

But she could do even more with medicine.

She sighed as she rolled paint on the wall.

It was annoying that the little medicine voice was always louder than the soothing painting voice.

She had the degree. One that others strived for, as Trace pointed out. It was within her reach to use it. If only.

If only what? If she wasn't such a coward? If she wasn't afraid of making a mistake?

She stepped back and bumped into the paint tray,

splashing paint on the floor. Grimacing, she grabbed a rag and wiped it up.

Mistakes were going to happen. She needed to deal with it. Grow some resilience and move on.

Or decide she was going to paint.

In a way she envied Trace. He knew what he wanted, and he went after it. She was still stalking his social media sites and couldn't believe what he posted that morning.

He was organizing a ball hockey tournament for Breaking Bread. Hattie must be thrilled. She was beyond grateful whenever a donation came their way. The tournament was scheduled for mid-April so Trace had a month to put it together. It was local, it was fun, and they could host it in a parking lot so their expenses would be minimal. It was a brilliant idea for a hockey town and a fundraiser for an excellent cause.

Would he let her help out? Talk to her? Give her heart back?

Margo rubbed her chest as heaviness settled in. She missed him.

Exasperated with herself, she rummaged through her tote bag and pulled out her cell phone. If she was about to do another go-round of ruminations, she wanted music to drown out the noise.

Chapter 32

Margo looked at the truck grill filling her rear-view mirror. Every few seconds, it inched closer. Not sure what he hoped to achieve. She was stuck at a red light. His impatient nudging wasn't going to make it change any faster. He'd better not bump her little red Spark with his antics. The last thing she wanted was to have to rent a yellow hatchback.

Finally the light changed to green, and Margo pulled away. It wasn't much farther to Breaking Bread, and she was relieved to pull in, put the car in park, and lock it up.

Hattie turned from the oven with a huge smile when Margo entered. If there was one constant Margo needed, it was Hattie's love. It radiated off Hattie like the sun, and Margo needed it like the air she breathed.

"Hello, honey. You look sun-kissed. Pretty miserable storm we had the other day. Did you make it home from your holiday before it hit?"

"We did, Hattie. I was all tucked inside before the ice came and the power went off. How did you make out here?"

"We were all cleaned up on Saturday before it started. Sunday we had sandwiches by candlelight. Pat's bakery didn't have the sales they expected and donated their bread to us. It was nice and fresh."

"Oh, how generous of them."

"Yes, everyone enjoyed it. Ate every last loaf," Hattie said with a laugh. She nodded to the dining room. "Ottie's back, and your boyfriend is with him."

"He's not really my boyfriend, Hattie, but I'm so happy to hear Ottie's back. That's great."

"Yes, he's doin' real well. The extra bit of pampering has done him a world of good. Why don't you go out and say hello before you start the washing up?"

Margo hesitated. "Are you sure? He's probably catching up with everyone."

Hattie nodded. "He is, that's for sure. But I'm certain he'd like to say hello."

Margo felt the burn of acid in her stomach. Waiting wasn't going to make it any easier. She turned and walked into the dining room. Carl sat in his usual spot, and she waved to him. "I'll bring your drink in a minute, Carl."

Carl nodded and waved and went back to talking with Angie.

At the sound of her voice, Trace turned in his chair.

Margo couldn't hold his gaze. She walked over, bent down, and squeezed Ottie's shoulders. "Ottie, it's so good to have you back."

"So good to be back," Ottie said, reaching up to pat the hand she rested on his shoulder.

"You gave us quite a scare. Don't do that again."

Ottie grinned and tipped his top hat. "Always good to change things up. Don't want to get too complacent."

"On the contrary. We like complacent." She looked over at Trace who was watching without a smile. "Hi, Trace."

He nodded. "Margo."

Ottie's glance ping ponged between Margo and Trace. "Trace here is practicing for his medical school interview. It's a week from Saturday."

"Congratulations, Trace. That's great," Margo said, trying to inject some enthusiasm.

Trace smirked. Maybe she missed the mark.

"Thanks," he said.

"Trace said it's something called MMR," Ottie continued.

"MMI, multiple mini-interviews," Trace corrected.

Ottie waved it away. "MMR. MMI. What's the

difference? The point is, he has to interview fake patients. He's trying to practice on me, but I told him to ask you. You're the expert."

Margo gave a crooked smile.

"You'll give him a few pointers, won't ya?" Ottie persisted.

"Of course," Margo lied. "I can help out. If he wants my help—"

"Of course he wants your help," Ottie said, glancing between her and Trace. He nudged Trace's elbow. "Don't ya?"

Trace jerked. "Oh yeah, of course. If she wants to help."

"What's the matter with you two? Of course she wants to help. You need help, and she can help you. There's nobody better." He fingered his hat. "But not right now. Right now I need you to get me some butterscotch ripple." He pointed at Trace. "But you need her help," he said sternly.

Trace laughed. "Okay. I'll get her help. And I'll get your ice cream. You're getting demanding in your old age."

Ottie laughed. "Oh, no. I've always been this way."

As Trace turned to go to the kitchen, Margo said, "I should get Carl's drink."

"Make a date," Ottie shouted.

Trace rolled his eyes. "Would you like to go out Friday night?"

Visions of the last gorgeous Friday night swam in her head.

"Dinner and a movie?" Trace asked.

Margo looked at him. "Sure, I'd like that."

"Oh," he said, snapping his fingers. "Actually there's a game on, and we have box tickets. How about dinner and a hockey game?"

She liked the idea of a movie better. Less talking. "Sure," she said reluctantly. "That sounds like fun."

Trace snorted at the tone of her voice. He moved out of earshot from Ottie. "If you'd rather not, I understand."

"No. It's okay. I can help."

Trace raised his eyebrows. "Okay. I'll pick you up at six on Friday."

Margo looked back at Ottie, who was looking pleased as punch.

Chapter 33

Margo looked at her reflection in the mirror and gave herself a pep talk.

All she had to do was get through the date tonight. Throw out some advice about the med school interview during dinner. Small talk through the hockey game. Shake his hand at the end of the evening and call it a day. After that, she could walk away. She could deal with her guilt on her own, in time. Walking away from Trace meant she wouldn't be constantly reminded of how her ineptness lurked just below the surface.

She took the time to straighten her hair and let it fall to her shoulders. She layered a white camisole under a red sweater and wound a thin red and black scarf around her neck. Go Cascades. Her tapered black jeans tucked neatly into warm leather boots.

Margo heard the knock on her door and squared her shoulders. Why did this feel worse than a trip to the dentist?

She plastered a fake smile on her face and opened the door. She wasn't absolutely sure, but his smile looked just as fake. He leaned in, as if he was going to greet her with a kiss, as he had so many times in the past, but then caught himself and jerked back.

Margo's heart tripped. Regret washed over her. If she could rewind the clock, she would. She so desperately wished she could. "I'll grab my coat," she said quietly, turning to open the closet.

Trace stepped inside and stuck his hands in his pockets. "Look, Margo, I feel like Ottie coerced you into this. If you'd rather not . . ."

"Are you cancelling our date?" Margo said, her eyes narrowed, her voice clipped.

Trace threw his hands up. "Not at all. I . . ."

"You what?"

"I want to make sure you know you can say no," he said finally, watching her face.

Margo slipped her arms in her coat and felt Trace reach over and help her with it. He ran his hand down her arm. Margo turned to face him and looked him in the eye. "Do you want to go out with me?" Images of his face – the disdain, the disappointment – flashed through her mind.

"Yes, I do."

She swallowed and her shoulders relaxed a little. "I want to go out with you."

Trace smiled slowly and took her hand. He leaned in and lightly kissed her lips. "Let's go."

After they settled into a cab, Margo looked over. "I've never seen you drive."

"I don't often need to. Everything's pretty handy within walking distance. Or I plan on drinking and don't want to drive afterward."

"What kind of car do you drive? You can tell a lot about a person by the car they drive."

"Is that so? What do you think I drive?"

She took her time answering. "Something fast and flashy."

He grinned. "So, I guess it's lucky I haven't picked you up in my beige station wagon?"

She burst out laughing. "You do not own a beige station wagon."

He glanced over at her. "And painters don't have medical degrees."

Margo sobered and looked at him ruefully. "Touché."

He squeezed her hand and was about to say something,

but the taxi pulled up to the restaurant, and Trace was distracted settling the fare.

The restaurant was a little bistro, a short walk from the arena.

"I thought this would be a bit quieter so we can talk," Trace said as he held the door open for her.

"Dr. MacMillan." A young woman, in a short black skirt and a loose-fitting floral top, walked over quickly. She grinned and reached out to shake Margo's hand.

"Clarisse. How are you?" She looks so much better, Margo thought. She'd gained weight, looked healthy. She tamed the anorexia monster.

"I'm great. I can't believe it's you. They told me at the clinic that you graduated, and I've been trying to find out where you went. Where's your practice?"

Margo grimaced silently. "I graduated, but I still have to do a residency. Right now, I'm taking a bit of time off."

"Oh," Clarisse said, frowning. "I really want to be your patient. You're the only one who's ever helped me. Can I give you my number and when you set up your practice you can call me?"

"That's not really–"

"Don't tell me I can't. I've been trying to find you since last summer." She grabbed a restaurant business card and wrote her name and number on the back. "Here, take it please. It would really mean a lot if you called me."

Margo took it reluctantly. "But you have a doctor in the meantime, right?"

Clarisse made a face. "I'm using the walk-in clinic for now. Call me," she said sternly.

Margo smiled at her.

"I'll show you to your table." Clarisse grabbed two menus. "I'll give you the best one," she whispered with a wink.

They were led to an intimate table near the window. A candle flickered beside a bud vase filled with a sprig of orchids.

"Thank you, Clarisse. This is lovely."

Clarisse set the menus down. "Alex will be your waiter. Enjoy. Call me," she said and walked away.

Trace took Margo's coat and hung it with his own on a hook nearby. They sat down, and Margo picked up a menu.

"A former patient?" Trace asked. "She sounds like Daniel. You could start a fan club."

Margo snorted. "Yeah." It was flattering for sure. Nice to hear that she'd helped. But it made her sad. She couldn't explain it. It was unsettling.

The waiter came to fill their water glasses and expertly flicked their linen napkins onto their laps. Margo glanced around the restaurant as Trace ordered.

The twenty or so tables were full, but conversations were muted and quiet music filled the air. Margo admired the watercolor paintings hanging around the room, an abstract, a sunset, a welcoming Inukshuk. She relaxed in the charming ambiance.

When the waiter left, Margo changed the subject. "Congratulations on getting an interview. You must be thrilled."

Trace shrugged. "Only one, though."

"One is all it takes."

"I suppose, but it'd be nice to have a buffer. So I could do a practice round before I take on the one I really want."

"It's never that ideal. Have they told you how the interview will be structured?"

"They said there'd be an individual interview with a physician and a second-year medical student, a group interview, and five mini-interviews with actor patients."

"Wow. They don't want to miss anything. At least you'll have a chance to sell yourself in the individual interview and show them how you work as part of a team with the group interview. I imagine the mini-interviews will be scenarios covering empathy and ethics."

"All in one neat package, one week from tomorrow."

"You've come along way, baby."

"I'd like to go a bit further. Any tips?"

The waiter served their drinks, a beer for Trace and a fruity cocktail for Margo.

She took a sip and slowly stirred it with the straw. "For the group interview, remember that you'll be assessed the whole time. Speak up and join in, but don't hog the conversation. Smile, look people in the eye. Don't joke around, but keep in line with the tone of the group.

"For the individual interview, prepare for the question 'Tell me about yourself.' Start with your undergrad and then highlight some of the projects you've been involved in. Link them to skills that would make you a good doctor, like you did for your essay. But be brief. Aim to cover three activities in about two to three minutes."

Trace nodded. "Like the tutoring, work at Breaking Bread . . ."

"The research project, organizing the ball hockey tournament. That's a fantastic idea, by the way."

Trace looked pleased. "Thanks. Ottie and Hattie are really into it. Hopefully, it'll raise some money to keep them in butterscotch ripple perpetuity."

Margo laughed.

The waiter set down plates artfully arranged with leafy greens, dried cherries, toasted walnuts, and topped with rounds of warm, melted goat cheese. Margo's mouth watered as she inhaled the sweet aroma of the raspberry vinaigrette.

They picked up their forks.

"What about the MMIs? What are they like?" Trace asked.

Margo took a mouthful of salad and enjoyed the combination of tart cherries with the crunch of walnut. She swallowed and wiped her mouth with the napkin. "You'll be given a scenario. Usually you have one or two minutes to read it over. Read it carefully, and focus on the task it asks you to do. An actor in the room will act out the scenario. Do your best to pretend it's real."

"Sounds straightforward," Trace said.

Margo nodded. "It might be something like 'your roommate asks if he can copy an assignment you've finished. It's due tomorrow.' When you get in there, they might throw at you that the roommate is depressed or has a medical issue that prevented him from getting his assignment done, or he wants to use yours to boost his mark."

Trace frowned. "What's the right answer?"

Margo sipped her drink. "I don't think there's necessarily a right or wrong answer. They want to see how you approach it. Did you find out what's going on, can you put yourself in their shoes—"

"Ah," Trace said, waving his fork. "Empathy."

"Yes. But don't agree to cheat. That's bad."

"Be patient and understanding, then rip the carpet out from underneath them."

Margo smirked. "Well, kinda yeah. But in the nicest possible way."

"Right," Trace said with a quick laugh.

Margo savored the last of the goat cheese as it melted in her mouth and set down her fork. "It could also be stuff like breaking bad news, telling an elderly patient that they have to give up their driver's license, or telling a truck driver who suffers from sleep apnea that he can't drive unless he uses a CPAP machine. Disclosing a medical error, ratting out a classmate who cheated, an assisted suicide scenario . . ."

"Should be a fun time," said Trace, taking a sip of beer.

The waiter removed their salad plates and set down their meals. Trace had ordered blackened chicken with roasted potatoes. The peppery spices wafted up and mixed with the citrus aroma of her orange glazed snapper.

Margo picked up her knife and fork. "I've seen you with Ottie and the others at Breaking Bread. You won't have any trouble."

Trace glanced at Margo, his eyebrows raised. "Thanks for the vote of confidence. It means a lot," he said in a serious tone.

"Most importantly, when you walk out of one room, put what you did completely out of your mind and focus on what's next. Stay in the moment."

"When I screw up, you mean."

Margo laughed and shook her head. She held up her glass to him. "I think Dr. Bennett has a nice ring to it."

Chapter 34

They walked to the arena, the air crisp, the snow lightly falling. In the still air, the snowflakes made their way leisurely to the ground.

Trace pulled a Cascades tuque from his pocket and put it on. He brushed a hand over her hair. "You straightened your curls."

Margo smiled. "For a change. But this snow may make them curly again."

They joined the throngs of people going into the arena but broke off at a narrow hallway leading to an elevator. Trace showed the attendant his box seat tickets, and they were whisked up to the fourth floor.

He checked his watch as he tried the door to the box. "I don't have a key, but my parents should be here already."

Margo froze. Her heart stopped beating, then went into overdrive. When Trace held the door for her, she couldn't move.

With the slightest pressure on the small of her back, Trace urged her through.

Three young men stood inside the door, each with a beer in their hand. Their faces lit up when they saw Trace.

"Trace, good to see you, buddy."

Trace shook hands with two of them and grinned at the third. "Managed to pull yourself away from the drawing board, did you?" Trace pulled Margo closer. "Margo, this is my brother, Jacob."

The resemblance was striking. Jacob had longer hair,

a darker blond, but shared the same square jaw and frosty blue eyes.

"And his friend, Luke, and my cousin, Chris."

"Pleased to meet you." Margo shook hands with all three.

"The fridge is well stocked," Jacob said, motioning toward a kitchenette with his beer. "Help yourself."

"You might need it, if you're cheering for the Cascades," Chris said with a laugh.

Luke turned to him. "You're going to get uninvited."

"Or pitched over the balcony," Trace added as he moved to get drinks for Margo and himself.

Margo accepted a beer from Trace and stood with the group. The four shared an easy camaraderie and good-natured teasing.

Margo's glance slid over to Trace's parents, sitting between two other couples in the cushioned seats overlooking the rink. They were engrossed in a lively conversation. Could she duck out unnoticed? Her stomach churned at the thought of meeting them.

"What do you do, Margo?" Chris asked.

Margo looked at him. "I'm a painter."

His eyebrows went up. "Cool. What medium?"

"Well, I paint a lot of walls," she said with a laugh. "But I also paint canvasses. Acrylic, oil, watercolor, I've dabbled in them all."

"Do you have a favorite?"

"Um, if I want to spend time, I prefer acrylic. But for something quick and light, I'd probably choose watercolor. Do you paint?"

"Not at all," he said with a laugh. "I'm an architect. All straight lines and angles."

"A different kind of art," Margo said with a smile.

"Trace, you're here," his mom said, stepping closer and wrapping her arms around Trace in a hug.

"Hi, Mom. We snuck in a few minutes ago." He kissed her cheek. "Mom, I want you to meet Margo MacMillan. Margo, my mom, Anita."

"It's lovely to meet you, Margo." Anita extended her hand to shake. "Are you a hockey fan?"

Margo nodded, her throat dry. "I . . . I don't get to the games very often, but I enjoy watching them."

Anita nodded. "We don't get to as many as we'd like, but the view from up here is spectacular. Although sometimes I've been tempted to listen to the play-by-play as we watch. I don't understand all the calls or the strategy behind the plays like the boys." She smiled at Trace, who had walked to the railing to watch the start of the game with the other men. "You know," she continued, "you look a bit familiar."

Margo's stomach roiled. Her heart, already racing, skipped a beat. She had a split second to decide whether to tell the truth. She took a breath. "Actually, we have met briefly. I was working at the hospital when your father died. I came to give you the news. I'm very sorry."

Anita's brow wrinkled. "That was you? I thought Trace mentioned you were a painter."

Margo felt like the room became airless. "I'm taking some time off from medicine. I worked in the hospital during my final year."

"Oh, I see," Anita said, looking at Margo closely. "That was all such a blur. Poor Dad. I was devastated at the time, but he had so many health problems, we shouldn't have been surprised. Funny, no matter how prepared you think you are, it still comes as a shock."

Margo nodded, staying silent.

"You know, you were the only one, the only doctor, to come and speak to me."

Margo frowned. "The surgeon didn't talk to you?"

Anita shook her head. "No, he didn't drop by at all. The nurses more or less took over and helped me with all the arrangements." She folded the corner of the napkin she held. "For what it's worth, I really appreciated you breaking the news to me."

Margo looked at her with wide eyes, and then looked away. "I felt terrible."

Anita nodded. "It was terrible. Nobody expected him to die so suddenly. He was so hopeful that the operation would work wonders."

Margo swallowed. She felt two feet tall. "That was probably my fault. I talked to him before the operation, and I reassured him that he would do well. That he'd be up and about in no time at all."

Anita looked at her and shook her head. "Well, we can't say he didn't know the risks. He'd been told to stop smoking, told to slow down the drinking, but he was stubborn. Said life wasn't worth living unless he was living it up." She sighed. "I think he appreciated the reassurance. He seemed a lot calmer, more peaceful when I spoke to him about the operation, and I don't think it would have changed the outcome." She rubbed Margo's shoulder.

Margo looked at her. "I wish the outcome had been different."

Anita nodded. "Me, too. And if he'd listened to the doctors twenty years ago, it would have been." She watched the group cheer as a goal was scored. "Enough of this sad talk. You'd probably like a break from medicine. I'm going to grab a soda for Gwen and myself. Go and enjoy the game with Trace."

Chapter 35

Margo turned to go and then stopped. "Gwen?"

Anita nodded and smiled. "My sister." She laughed. "I'm still wrapping my tongue around that. I've known I had a sister for a few years, but we've only connected recently."

Margo felt a weight lift from her shoulders. Anita knew about Gwen.

Later that night, lying in bed, Margo thought about Trace's mom. There was a woman who was generous and kind. *She* would have made an excellent doctor. Trace was lucky, and if he had half of his mom's grace and goodness, he'd be fine.

Rose had told Anita about Gwen shortly after Trace's birth. Anita had given a crooked smile. She had been sworn to secrecy, had to dampen her fierce curiosity and longing to meet Gwen, unless Trace needed an organ transplant. Jeez. But when her father died and Gwen was mentioned in the will, she had tracked her down. Anita and Gwen now shared a close bond, like they'd known each other forever.

Go figure. The route was a little circuitous, but the destination the same.

The ache of guilt in Margo's chest eased a bit. It was a start, but would she ever feel like a doctor? Would the inside ever match the outward façade?

She sighed, rolled over onto her side, and hugged her pillow.

She knew the stuff. That was the frustrating part.

She could rattle off the latest research and create a

decent differential. Common things were common. She'd memorized every management algorithm known to medicine.

And it hadn't helped. Patients didn't present with the common. They were all over the map. Where was the pattern? Where was the branch on the algorithm for all the 'what ifs?'

The simple bladder infection in the patient with only one kidney. The diabetic with gangrene in his toe who refuses the amputation. The patient prepped and ready for surgery who has a cardiac arrest and dies.

Where was the branch on the algorithm for that? There was no branch. It was a scary leap off the branch into *I hope to hell I'm right*.

She rolled onto her back, stared at the ceiling, and sighed deeply.

How could she do it? There was so much uncertainty. There was so much more.

Which was what a residency was for, she thought as she hugged the pillow closer. And look at Clarisse. She'd have at least one patient eager to see her.

She drew the comforter up around her, tucking it under her chin. In the dim light, she caught a glimpse of the painting hanging on the wall. It was one of the few of her own gracing her apartment, and painting it hadn't really been a straight path either. It had started out as a simple white winter landscape and morphed into an autumn vista with rich burnt yellow and orange against a shimmering blue lake. The white wouldn't stick.

That was art. It was unpredictable. You could follow what felt right and go with it. Something better usually came from it. In the end, she'd hung the painting in her bedroom because she loved waking up to the vibrant colors and the season of change within the constant of nature that it represented.

Art. She had learned to accept unpredictability in painting. It was fundamental to creativity.

Why was it so hard to accept the unpredictability in medicine? She had the science of medicine down pat. Now she had to adjust to the art. Patients weren't going to come in tidy little packages following preset algorithms. They were going to be unique. She had to adjust and figure out what was best, even if it meant coloring outside the lines or thinking outside the box. No matter how uncomfortable it felt for her, something better might come from it.

A burning pain flared in her gut. If she was going to revisit her medical degree, she should also get stocks in antacids.

Was it worthwhile getting up and getting something for the pain or should she try to sleep it off? Margo glanced at the clock. Just after midnight, already Saturday. Another weekend and halfway through March.

Margo sat up, wide-awake. Shit. March fourteenth was her mother's birthday. She should have called her. They weren't best friends by any stretch of the imagination, but they never missed a birthday.

What time would it be there? Her mom was three hours behind. 9 p.m. Not too late.

Margo threw back the covers and turned on the bedside light. She grabbed a big sweater, slipped her arms in, and wrapped it around her. She pulled on thick fleece socks, and turning lights on as she went, padded into the living room. She picked up her phone, settled into the sofa, and with a fortifying breath, dialed her mom's number.

"Hello?"

Margo's heart pulled at the sound of her mom's voice. "Mom. Happy Birthday."

"Margo," her mom said softly. "You called."

Margo felt a lump gather in her throat. A gauge of her stress level. Her mother hadn't made her sentimental in over three years.

"I wanted to wish you Happy Birthday."

"Well that's lovely. It's lovely that you called. Thank you."

That was a first. A bit strange. "Is everything okay?" Margo asked.

"Of course, dear. It's late for you, and I didn't think you'd call. I hear you're having quite the icy winter."

The weather. The weather was safe.

"Yeah, it's been cold. But hopefully we're at the end of it now. How about you? Is your garden blooming already?"

She listened to her mother's voice, stronger now as she chatted about the familiar. The crocuses and the tulips blooming, the cherry blossoms starting.

"How are things with you?" her mother asked, finally.

Margo never knew if her mother really wanted to know or if she asked out of politeness. "Good. Things are good. Work is busy."

"Well, that's good. I figured you were busy. I tried to call last week, but I didn't get through."

Margo was taken aback. She tried to call? "Really? I missed that. Did you leave a message?"

"No, no. It wasn't urgent. I had a medical question. I know you don't like to talk about medicine, but . . ."

"Mom."

"Well, I didn't like to ask," her mom said defensively. "Whenever I mention something about medicine, it seems to upset you."

Margo shook her head. "Mom, you hardly took an interest when I was going through school. I thought you didn't want me to talk about it. I thought it made you mad."

Her mother was silent.

"Mom?"

"Oh, Margo," her mother said, her voice shaking. "I wasn't mad." Margo heard her sigh through the phone. "I wasn't mad. I was sad."

"Sad? Why?"

"I was worried, especially when you were accepted. Medical school is so expensive. I didn't have that kind of money. When your dad died, it was all I could do to keep a roof over our head and food on the table. There was no room for extras. You were only two years away from finishing your degree, and I had just enough saved for that. I couldn't afford a medical degree."

"But Mom, I didn't ask you to help pay for it."

"I know. But I wanted to. I thought I should."

Margo scoffed impatiently.

"It seemed like such a pipe dream. Medical school. You'd have to work so hard. You were already a talented artist. Why put yourself through that?" her mother added.

"You never said any of this to me," Margo said.

"You were so excited. I couldn't."

"I thought you were mad. I didn't understand why."

"I'm sorry, Margo. I truly am. Here I was, worried about how hard it would be for you, and I've only made it harder. You never once asked for money," she said, censure in her voice.

"You didn't have the money to lend. I knew that. I didn't expect you to."

"I can't tell you how proud I am of you," her mother said slowly. "M.D. Gold medal."

Margo was silent. Her eyes filled at the words she hadn't heard before.

"Talented artist. Smart businesswoman. I was at lunch with some friends last week. I mentioned you, and I was told that one of your paintings is hanging in the lobby of the Heritage House. The Heritage House, Margo. Did you know that?"

Margo laughed. "Yeah, I knew."

"Why didn't you tell me?"

"There's one at Top Flight, too."

"I'm writing it down. I'll have to make a trip there, as well."

"I can send you a picture," Margo offered.

"No. I want to see the real thing. June didn't know about that one."

Margo shifted and tucked her legs up underneath her. "Did you get the medical question answered? The one you were calling about?"

"Oh, that was for June, too. She had a double mastectomy five years ago. Her mother had breast cancer at forty, and June has that cancer gene they talk about."

"BRAC 1 or 2."

"Yes, something like that. Anyway, they found a lump in her chest wall."

"Oh, no."

"Yes. I was calling to ask if it could be cancer. I mean, I thought, how could it? They removed the whole breast. There was nothing left to get cancer in."

"Unfortunately, you can get cancer in the chest wall, even after a mastectomy. It's not common, but possible."

"Oh." Her mother sighed. "Poor June. She goes this week for more tests. I hope it's not."

"I hope so too, Mom. There are other possibilities. It may just be a cyst in her skin or extra tissue in the scar."

"I'll let her know," her mother said. "Even the slightest bit of reassurance will help her. She's so worried, and her doctor didn't give her much information. You really don't mind me asking? I thought medicine was taboo."

"No, it's fine. It was taboo because I thought it upset you."

"Oh. I thought it was taboo because you dropped out."

"I didn't drop out, Mom. I'm taking a year off to figure out if I want to make a career out of it."

"Or paint?"

"Yeah."

"Why don't you do both? My doctor only works part-time. I have to wait a week to get an appointment, for goodness sake. You could do that."

Margo considered. "I suppose I could. I'm not sure if I like medicine enough."

"If you're good enough," her mother corrected.

"Well, yes, I guess," Margo said with a sigh.

"Margo, you earned the gold medal. You're good enough. You have to start believing in yourself. You were always the one your friends turned to when they needed advice. You'll make a wonderful doctor. Don't stop for the wrong reasons." Her mother paused. "I wish I could give you a hug."

"I wish you could too, Mom," Margo said huskily.

"For my birthday present, I'd like to come and visit you." Her mother paused. "What's going on with June got me thinking, and June said she would travel with me. She knows a bed and breakfast where we could stay. We can do the touristy things while you're working, and we could have dinner with you. Spend some time with you. What do you think?"

Margo smiled. "I think that's a wonderful idea."

"We'll wait until the weather is better. We don't want to travel in an ice storm. And after June's tests, of course. But we'll count on her getting a clean bill of health, and then we'll book our tickets."

"I'd like that, Mom. It's been a long time. I can send some money for you."

Her mother was silent. "That's not necessary, dear, but thank you for the lovely offer." Her voice shook. She cleared her throat.

"Happy Birthday, Mom."

"Thanks. We'll see you soon."

Margo hung up the phone. She wrapped the sweater tighter and set the phone on the table. After all these years, her mother wanted to visit. Her mother was proud of her. A warm feeling washed over her, and she smiled. Her mother was proud of her.

Margo leaned back against the sofa. Could she do it? Finish medicine? Learn the art? She wouldn't have to give up painting completely. Maybe she could keep what makes her happy, continue to do what fulfills her, and find a balance.

Margo reached over and shut off the light. She made her way to her bedroom and snuggled under the covers.

Her mom was proud of her.

She wiped the tears from her eyes.

Chapter 36

Trace looked around the room at the seven other medical school hopefuls who, like him, had drawn the group interview first.

He hadn't seen so many people dressed in black since his grandfather's funeral. All of them had some variation of a black jacket and white shirt with conservative dark ties for the men. Except for pink bow tie dude. Seriously?

They sat at a round table in a tight room. The gray-tinted window, filling one wall, reflected like a mirror. They weren't told they were being observed, but hello. Of course, they were. A few obviously missed that memo. No smiles. No eye contact. They said nothing.

They needed Margo's coaching.

They started with cursory introductions. He half listened, his mind busy planning what to say. He got his name right – so far, so good.

Next up, they were given a topic to discuss. Doctor-assisted suicide. Jump right into controversy. The silence was painful.

"I think there are two sides of the coin to consider with assisted suicide," Trace began, making eye contact with the ones who looked up. "Part of dying with dignity should include the right to choose to die. The elderly who have lived full lives and develop a debilitating illness, the terminally ill in severe pain." He shrugged. "They should have the right to decide to die peacefully, when they choose. On the other hand, you have to consider the potential for abuse – the children who want the inheritance money, the family who can't afford the care. Just as difficult would be the ones who are ill and have lost hope, like the patient who's depressed or the patient with cancer pain, but who have the potential to recover. The question comes down to who should have the final say. I think that each case would have to be considered carefully to make sure the underlying motives are in the right place."

"I completely disagree," said Pink Bow Tie. "It should never be allowed, under any circumstances. A doctor's role is to help people, not kill them."

No one else spoke. Trace looked around. Should he jump in again? Margo said not to hog the floor, but Pink Bow Tie stared at him, his face set.

"It's a difficult decision. What if the most helpful thing is to let them die as they wish?" Trace asked when no one else spoke up.

"It's not right," insisted Pink Bow Tie.

"I think it should be allowed in special cases," said a redhead. All the heads swiveled to her, and she blushed and looked down.

Trace almost jumped in, but Pink Bow Tie couldn't let it go.

And so it continued for another fifty minutes. They debated whether experimental drugs should be released to fight the Ebola virus outbreak, discussed the pros and cons of legalizing marijuana – surprisingly strong views on that one, thought Trace – and what should be done for doctors who were addicted to drugs. Trace suppressed a grin. Interesting choice of topic on the heels of legalizing marijuana.

As they wrapped up, Trace considered the candidates. Pink Bow Tie needed to take it down a notch. Redhead needed to pump the brakes. Speak up more. And not let Pink Bow Tie railroad her.

He thought he did okay. Tried to chip in, take a stand and

not sit on the fence, listened, commented. If they marked on eye contact and e-quotient, he should be fine.

Trace had a half-hour break to eat lunch, which the school provided. It wasn't a bad spread, but there weren't many hearty appetites.

He stood off to one side and ate a roast chicken and cheese sub. Carefully. Last thing he needed was a grease stain on his tie. As he finished, he caught a glimpse of a familiar face. "Russ, how's it going?" Trace asked, stretching out his hand.

Russ leaned over and shook it. "Not bad, man. Not bad. Haven't seen you for a while. You're not hanging in the Sci-Fi lounge any more?"

Trace grinned. Those were the days. "On to bigger and better things."

"More comfortable chairs in the math department?" Russ asked.

"Absolutely. And highly caffeinated drinks in the drink machine."

"How do they keep that a secret?"

"We write a complicated math equation on the exterior. Drives mere mortals away."

Russ laughed. "I would be among them. Running, not walking." He crumpled up the paper wrapper from his sub and tossed it in the trash. "So you're thinking of medicine. They could use more math brains like you," Russ said.

"I'm hoping. Are you interviewing anywhere else?"

"Brighton last week and U of S in two weeks' time."

Trace nodded. "Nice. Congrats. How does this compare to Brighton?"

"They're all about the same. Smile, nod, try to keep the 'how the hell is this relevant' look off my face. Play the game."

Trace grinned. Russ would make a great doctor. "Good luck with it."

An elderly woman with a clipboard walked into the room and called their names to begin the next round.

Russ reached out to shake Trace's hand. "Hopefully I'll see you again on the first day of classes."

Trace shook his hand. "Save me a seat in the front row."

They followed the woman out into the hallway. Russ was shepherded to the personal interview, and Trace followed the group for the MMI. There were five stations, each ten minutes long, with two minutes to read the scenario and eight minutes to interact with an actor patient.

Trace stood outside the door of the first room and read the instructions.

You have one dose of a life-saving drug and two patients who need it. One patient is the two-year-old child of a physician and her husband. The second patient is a sixty-seven-year-old scientist who developed the vaccine for HIV.

In the next eight minutes please initiate a discussion with your colleague about whom you will choose to treat.

Trace took a deep breath. Okay. Think. What would Margo want to know?

The practical stuff. Do both parties want it? Any other options? Could the child take a lower dose and they share it? Could they get more drug from another country? How sick are they? His heart rate slowed as he came up with reasonable ideas.

When the chime sounded for him to enter the room, he walked in with a smile and introduced himself.

And the fun began.

He asked his practical questions and when the chime ended the interview, he thanked the 'colleague' and wondered how the hell anyone would make a decision like that. Both patients needed and wanted it, there were no other options, and both should get it. There would be no good ending to that story. Set it aside, he told himself, hearing Margo's voice. He did the best he could, and it's done.

He walked over to the next room and read the scenario.

There are two parts to the next section. You will share your decision with the two patients involved. In the first interview you will speak to the mother of the two-year-old child, and in the second interview you will speak to the scientist. You may only give the drug to one patient. Each interview will be eight minutes long.

Holy shit. Trace felt sweat run down his back between his shoulder blades.

He hadn't made a decision. He had gathered information. How could he choose to end someone's life? And tell them to their face?

Thirty seconds. Shit. Who gets it?

When the chime sounded, he wiped damp palms on his pants and walked into the room to greet 'the mother.'

The next sixteen minutes were the longest of his life. His mouth was so dry, he stumbled and stuttered. He felt the sweat on his brow and feared it might drip off his chin. It got worse when the patient looked sympathetic. He was pretty sure that wasn't a good sign. That's when he perspired through his suit jacket.

Shit. Guess he could kiss medicine good-bye. That was dismal.

He floated through the last two scenarios. Couldn't even recall what he said, what he did.

When it was over, he sighed deeply. He needed a drink. Water and sugar for now. Something stronger later.

Next up was the personal interview.

Put it behind you, Trace. He looked around at the other devastated expressions and took some consolation that it wasn't just him. They all sucked. They must have put all the B-list players in the same pool.

Move on, he told himself.

Focus on what's next.

A doctor and a second-year medical student sat across from him. They introduced themselves briefly and then turned to him.

"Tell us a bit about yourself," the doctor said, with a smile.

Thank you, Margo.

Trace talked briefly about his undergrad degree, graduate work, his tutoring, the research he was doing, and his experience volunteering at Breaking Bread. "I've organized a ball hockey tournament to raise money for Breaking Bread. Three weekends from now. There was a lot of interest, and we had to cap it at sixteen teams. But it would be nice if it became an annual event and grew," Trace finished.

The medical student grinned. "I'll be there. We entered a team."

Trace smiled. "No kidding? That's great." He nodded. Small break there.

The doctor was very interested in Trace's research. She had a project of her own on the go and asked Trace about multivariate analysis of variance versus analysis of variance with Tukey's HSD post-hoc testing. The great thing about knowing the ins and outs of statistical analysis was simplifying it. And generally nobody's life was at stake.

At the end of the interview, Trace smiled, shook their hands, and thanked them.

Done and done. At least the interview went better than the MMIs. So if he wasn't totally sunk with his MMI score, he may have a chance.

He shook his head. Was medicine really like that? Did doctors have to make those tough decisions? He hadn't thought it would come up that often, but really, organ donation, blood transfusions, limited drugs, all the extra care people had to pay for, it probably wasn't as rare as he imagined.

No wonder Margo had a hard time. She'd care too much. She had such goodness in her, was beautiful to the core. It would break her heart to make a decision like that. And break her spirit.

And who would she talk to about it? Another doctor, probably. She'd need someone with a similar perspective.

He'd be useless. He couldn't even get through the interview. Hell, with actors. He was sweating bullets, and it wasn't even real.

Thank goodness she chose painting. Because if she ever decided to go back to medicine, that would be the end of any relationship with him. She'd need a doctor.

He owed Margo a bucketload of thanks and an apology. If only he could rewind the clock and take back what he'd said to her when Ottie was sick. Throw a little empathy out there.

How could he make it up to her? His body stirred at the thought of another Friday night.

He should probably start with an apology.

Chapter 37

Margo breathed in the fresh clean air of spring. Perfect day for Trace's ball hockey tournament. It was warmer, and the weather forecasters were pretty sure the last of the winter storms were finished. She hoped so. She was so ready for brighter clothes and fewer layers.

She threw her purse and jacket on the front seat beside her and settled into her car. Her car. With a brand spanking new paint job and shiny new windshield. It was so good to have it back. The Spark was great, but there was nothing like zooming around in her zippy little Mini-Coop.

She made a left-hand turn.

The last two weeks had been quiet. Painting was slow. The hotel job had finished, and the new homes weren't quite ready, so she and Chloe had a few days off.

Lots of painting-on-canvas time. Lots of thinking time. She'd even talked to her mom. Surprise, surprise. Not sure what had changed, but she decided not to analyze it and instead just enjoy it.

The big news? She had decided to go back to medicine.

Her gut clenched, and she took a deep breath and exhaled slowly. Obviously still a frisson of doubt there, but . . . she missed it.

Family medicine was a two-year residency. She'd invest the time and energy to get her license and then see. If she still had doubts, she could paint, or even practice medicine part-time and paint. Combine the best of both worlds. She rested her hand on her stomach. Even though there was a tiny bit of terror mixed in, too.

She stopped at a red light and tapped the steering wheel. Really, she could have walked to the ball hockey tournament, but it crossed her mind that a car might be handy in case of an injury. Not that Trace had asked her, but if nothing else, she could offer to help with the first aid.

Actually, she had debated whether to show up at all. It sounded like Trace had everything under control, from what she'd heard from Hattie and Ottie. They were brimming with excitement and couldn't stop chatting about it.

She, on the other hand, was less enthusiastic. It was a great cause. She knew she should support it. But she didn't want to see Trace.

Well, she did. But she didn't.

In the end, she decided to go, offer to help, and aim to stay out of Trace's way.

Trace. Her heart twisted. After his interview, he had sent flowers with a short note of thanks. The flowers had been beautiful. She'd babied them so they'd last and finally had to throw them out two days ago. But it had been weird reading the words on the card written in someone else's handwriting. Instead of Trace's voice in her head, someone else's popped up between them. She sighed. That was silly, but she longed to hear him again.

She pressed her lips together. He hadn't called. He hadn't texted. There was no excuse for her to see him now that his interview was done. He was playing the waiting game. She grimaced. Her too, but for a different reason.

She was waiting to see if he would call.

She pulled into the parking lot and her eyes widened. Trace didn't go halfway.

A huge tent, with a Breaking Bread banner, was set up in front of two rinks. The rinks were back to back and framed in knee-high boards around the periphery. Tall fences probably twice her height, towered between the rinks and behind the nets at the opposite ends.

Had she really been worried that no one would go? The place was packed. Kudos to Trace.

People milled about. Players registered at a table at one end of the tent. Teams of four in matching jerseys, with the goalies in full ice hockey gear, were waiting for their turn to play at the edge of the rink. Ottie, in his big top hat, sat on a high stool beside the registration desk, surrounded by an enthusiastic crowd.

Opposite, Hattie was busy handing out hot drinks. "Coffee or hot chocolate?" Hattie shouted above the din of the crowd as Margo approached.

Not waiting for an answer, Hattie handed her a cup. "Free coffee, courtesy of Tim Hortons. You here to help, baby girl?" she asked with a smile.

"Absolutely." Margo took a sip. "They donated this?"

"Yessiree. Coffee and hot chocolate from Tim Hortons, sandwiches from A Slice Above, and free homemade cookies."

"Wow, a feast. What can I do?"

"Smile and help me serve it up."

Tim Hortons dropped off half a dozen jugs of Gatorade for the players and had to refill the coffee twice during the morning. It was a big hit.

They had a steady stream of customers. Their generosity was heartwarming, and Margo thanked every one of them for their support.

And she watched Ottie. Every half hour, when the games finished, he hopped down from his stool and recorded the scores on a huge white board under the tent. The rest of the time, she could only see a sliver of his top hat in the center of the crowd surrounding him.

"What's with all the commotion around Ottie? What's he doing?" Margo asked Hattie during a lull.

"Signing autographs."

"Autographs?"

"You're not goin' believe it, but Ottie played hockey with the Shields."

"No." She turned wide eyes to Hattie.

Hattie laughed. "Four seasons as a professional. No wonder he's watching all them games. It's his ole stomping ground. And look at the love they're showering on him."

"Wow. He never said anything? He looks like he's having a blast."

"His time in the spotlight," Hattie said with a smile.

As the morning moved into the afternoon, the sunshine came out, and the temperature went up. A slight breeze helped cool the players.

By the time the teams narrowed to eight, then to four, and down to the final two, the tent and all the standing room only spots around the boards were full. Spectators cheered with each whistle. Young adults, families, and a few folks with a sprinkling of gray hair, crowded around the boards to watch the games. The fans were close enough to hear the players as they called out plays or banged their sticks for a pass. The four on four games were fast, with the players running and passing as they covered the rink from net to net.

The last game was tied as the clock ticked down the final forty seconds. With only twenty seconds left, the more aggressive team pushed passed the defense and deked the goalie, sliding a backhand shot past his pads. A horn sounded with the goal, and all the fans in blue and white jumped and clapped and high-fived their neighbor. The players, winded and sweaty, grinned and slapped each other on the back.

"Let's get this done," said the winger.

They set up at the centerline until the other team brought

the ball out from behind the goal line. Ten seconds later, the whistle blew and the game was over.

The noise from the fans escalated until the players finished shaking hands.

Trace took a microphone at the center of the rink and addressed the crowd. "Congratulations to the Sharp Shooters on their win. Well played. And of course, the big winner today is Breaking Bread. Thanks to everyone who helped out, made donations of food and drink, of their time and, of course, their money. Every little bit helps and will go a long way. Thanks to our special guest, Ottie Blakeman. I'll invite him to center rink to hand out the medals to the winning teams. Thanks again everyone. We hope to see you here again next year!"

Ottie stepped forward and handed out medals to the top three teams, with more handshakes and smiles.

Margo and Hattie cleared the table. The leftovers were packed up for Breaking Bread, and the rental company was standing by to take down the tent.

Just as they finished putting the last of the food away, Trace hurried past. "We're all heading out for pizza at The Melting Pot. You in?" he shouted to Hattie and Margo.

Hattie laughed. "Oh, no. These old bones have had enough. I'll drop by Breaking Bread to make sure everything is under control, but then I'm home for a hot bath, a quiet night, and a deep sleep. Let me give you a hug." She walked over and embraced Trace. "You're a good boy. Today was a huge success." She nodded over to Ottie. "In so many ways."

Trace leaned back and followed her gaze. "Do you think I'll be able to pull him away?"

"Might be the hardest part of the day," Hattie said with a laugh.

Trace looked over at Margo. "You'll come, right?"

Margo hesitated and then smiled. "Sure. That'd be fun."

Trace gave a thumbs-up. "Great. We're meeting there in half an hour." He strode away, calling out instructions to the last of the crew as he went.

Hattie turned to Margo. "You go and show that boy a good time," she said with a firm nod.

Margo smiled weakly. Hattie's definition of a good time and Trace's might be slightly different.

Chapter 38

Margo walked up to the entrance of The Melting Pot as Trace arrived.

"Oh, hi," Margo said, startled. "I thought you'd be inside already."

"I ran Ottie home first. He was losing altitude."

"What a day for him."

Trace nodded. "He loved it." He held the door open for her. "After you."

They walked in and spotted the rest of the crew sitting at a table. Trace waved to them, grabbed Margo's hand, and pulled her toward the table.

Margo had met the others briefly during the day when she brought them coffee and cookies. The men had been organizing the teams and refereeing, and the two women had looked after registration and timekeeping. Trace introduced her again and held the chair for her to sit beside him.

They ordered pizza and pitchers of beer and snacked on roasted garlic bruschetta while they waited. They were floating on the success of the day, and the conversation was lively.

"How much do you think you raised, Trace?" Rob asked. He was the shortest of the bunch, and as a referee, had probably run eight times that of the players.

Trace shrugged. "Dunno for sure, but I figure around six or seven grand."

Rob whistled. "That much. That's impressive."

Trace raised his glass. "To all the fantastic help today. Couldn't have done it without the team effort."

They clinked glasses and congratulated Trace for a smoothly run, successful day.

The pizza arrived and they dug in.

Conversations started around them, so Margo turned to Trace. "Thank you very much for the flowers, Trace. You didn't have to do that, but they were beautiful."

Trace finished chewing and wiped his mouth. "You're welcome. Thanks for all your help. It really made a difference. I could hear your voice throughout the day, whispering advice."

Margo smiled. "How did it go?"

Trace shrugged. "The group and one-on-one interviews went well, I thought. The MMIs were terrible."

Margo made a sound to contradict.

"No really. It was awful." He described the scenario. "There was no good way to end that."

Margo shook her head sympathetically. "There really isn't. It was probably more about how you approached it. Showing empathy when you had to break bad news. Exploring what the patient understood. It's actually a good scenario because you have to talk with a colleague and give good news and bad." She raised her eyebrows. "Wouldn't be easy though."

"No. Anyhow, it's done. The research project I joined won a huge grant, and I've been offered a full-time position for a year. So if it doesn't work out with medicine, at least I have something to fall back on."

"That's great. Congrats about the grant. When do the medical school offers go out?"

"May second. All the schools send out emails at the same time."

Margo nodded. "That hasn't changed." She took a sip of beer. "That's the same day I find out about the residency."

"The residency?"

Margo looked at him. "I've decided to go back."

Trace sat back with a start. "Back? Back to medicine?"

Margo nodded. "I decided to give it another try." She sighed and shifted her beer mug, wiping the water ring with her napkin. "I've applied to family medicine."

"What about your painting?" Trace asked with wide eyes.

Margo looked at him, surprised. She expected him to be grinning, telling her that there was no question she should go back. "I'll still do that part-time. I don't want to give it up completely. I couldn't. But Chloe wants to take on more responsibility. I'll do what I can during the two years of residency, and then I'm hoping I'll be able to balance medicine with painting." She shrugged. "I'll try it."

"Wow," Trace said, raising his hands. "That's great." He reached for his beer. "You know, I was thinking of you when I finished the MMIs. I realized I owed you an apology."

Margo looked at him, puzzled.

"I got a small taste of how difficult medicine could be with that case. I shouldn't have said what I did at the hospital with Ottie." He looked at her with sad eyes. "I'm sorry I gave you a hard time." He gulped his beer. "But this is great news."

Margo's stomach pain flared. "What happened with Ottie was a bit different." She forced herself to make eye contact. "Trace, I knew your grandfather."

"Really? How?"

"I met him at the hospital. I sat down with him and had a conversation about how the procedure was relatively minor. I reassured him he would do fine."

Trace stared at her. "That was you?"

Margo nodded silently. She wiped the table again and folded the napkin. "I felt terrible when he died. I misled him. I let him down. It must have been hard on your whole family."

Trace looked at her thoughtfully. "Yes, and no. He knew he was at risk for a heart attack. He had been told that for years and ignored it." He shrugged. "Is that why you couldn't talk to Ottie?"

She nodded. "I was afraid I would say something to make it worse. I felt awful, but I couldn't bring myself to talk to him. I'm sorry."

Trace covered her hand with his. "Hey, it's okay. Ottie understood. He was totally cool with it. I was the one who was out of line. I'm sorry for making you feel like you did something wrong." Trace squeezed her hand. "You'll be fantastic. Medicine needs you."

Margo smiled weakly. "You'll be fantastic, too. I hope you get in."

Trace looked at her. More than ever, he hoped so too.

Chapter 39

Trace sat at the island in his kitchen finishing a bowl of Cap'n Crunch. He eyed his computer. It held his future.

The offers were sent out at 8 a.m. It was now ten. He hadn't set his alarm. He wasn't in a hurry to find out because if he didn't get in, well, he didn't want to think about it. He finished the last scoop of cereal and took another sip of coffee. Fortifying sugar and caffeine.

If he didn't get in.

He gave a large sigh. If he didn't get in, it would really, really suck.

He'd tried to keep a bit of distance from Margo. When she told him she was going back to start a family medicine residency, it felt like someone took a sledgehammer to his heart. He couldn't compete with that. He wouldn't be any good to her. He realized he loved her. She was everything he'd ever need, but she would need more. What was that saying, 'if you loved someone, set them free?' Or some such shit.

He rubbed his chest absently. He had tried to keep his distance to see if that would help. It hadn't. He had seen her at Breaking Bread, of course. On the Tuesday after the ball hockey tournament, he had dried dishes while she washed. He loved her quick wit, the way she saw the world, her goodness, her patience. He loved the way her curls got curlier as she stood over the hot water. His body stirred as he pictured her naked, reflected in the glass with his arms around her.

He shook himself impatiently. Remembering shit like

that wasn't going to help. If he didn't get into medical school, he would have to walk away.

He took another sip of coffee.

Okay Bennett, get it done. Open the freakin' computer.

Trace wiped damp palms on his trackpants and opened his laptop. He punched in his password.

Please wait while we update windows. Do not shut off your computer.

Holy fuck.

Three agonizing minutes later, it was one hundred percent complete.

He clicked on his email and waited for the new mail to download.

Cantech University Congratulations! You have been accepted . . .

He hopped off the bar stool and leapt up, punching the air with his fist. "Yes!" He raised both hands in the air and jumped again.

He took a deep breath and tried to slow his racing heart. "Yes." He perched on the edge of the bar stool and opened the email.

He was in. There it was in beautiful black and white. How sweet was that. Yes. He did it. He punched the air again.

He needed to tell Margo.

It was Friday. She should be painting at the new development his father was building. He had to see her. He had to tell her in person.

He did it. He got in. He was going to be a doctor.

He shut his computer with a click and finished the last of his coffee.

Life was good. He jumped again.

He changed into a T-shirt and jeans, grabbed the keys to his car, and headed out.

Trace pulled into the makeshift parking lot in front of the site trailer at the new development.

Inside, a foreman leaned against the wall, sipping a coffee. Trace greeted the secretary sitting at the desk. "Is Margo MacMillan around? Painting?"

The secretary checked the schedule. "She is. Number eighty-two, fourth on the left," she said, eyeing him curiously.

Trace smiled. "Thanks."

He walked the short distance feeling like he was floating on air. Yes. He was in. It was singing in his head.

He opened the front door of the bungalow and stepped inside.

She was painting in the foyer and turned to look when the door opened. In paint-spattered shorts and T-shirt, her hair pinned up, loose curls that just couldn't be tamed framing her face, her blue eyes lighting up when she saw him, she was beautiful. Simply beautiful.

"I got in," he said.

She gasped. "Congratulations!" She set the brush down and jumped into his waiting arms. "Congratulations, Trace," she whispered in his ear.

He held her tight and breathed deeply. His world tilted. Everything felt right. He pulled back and smiled at the tears shimmering in her eyes.

"I'm so excited for you," she said, with a watery smile.

He laughed and pressed his lips to her. She met him hungrily. Their tongues danced and his lips tasted. He savored the sweetness.

He pulled back to look her in the eyes. "I had to share it with you first. I know I've said this a million times, but I couldn't have done it without you. Thank you." He caught her lips in a gentle kiss. "I have to go tell my folks, but you'll celebrate with me tonight?"

Margo smiled. "I'd love to, but won't your parents want to celebrate with you?"

"I'll save another night for them. Tonight, I want to be with you."

She reached out and hugged him close. "I'd love that."

"I'll pick you up at home. Seven o'clock?"

"Sounds perfect."

After another quick kiss, he turned to go. She reached out and squeezed his hand. "Dr. Bennett. Wow."

He laced his fingers with hers and grinned.

He left her reluctantly and strode to his car. He had a lot to do before seven.

Chapter 40

Trace knocked on Margo's door and smiled when he saw the shadow cross the peephole. See, he was a good influence. She pulled open the door, and he leaned in to kiss her. He would never tire of it.

"I wasn't sure how to dress," she said, looking at his slacks and dress shirt. "Is this okay?"

Trace looked at the soft flowy dress that hugged her curves and left her long legs bare to mid-thigh, her feet in dainty gold sandals. "You look beautiful."

Her shoulders relaxed. "Thank you. You look incredibly hot."

Trace laughed. "What I was after," he said. He held her sweater while she locked the door and slipped his hand in hers as they made their way outside.

"I guess I'll finally see your car?" she asked, squeezing his hand.

He looked at her and then nodded at the limousine waiting at the curb. "We're celebrating, so I snagged the company limo again."

The driver opened the door, and Margo climbed in and adjusted her dress. Trace sat beside her and handed her a glass of champagne. "To you Margo, beautiful, gifted, and generous."

Margo held up her glass. "To you Trace, brilliant and dedicated with a huge heart. Congratulations."

They clinked glasses and sipped.

Margo swallowed and then looked at him with shining

eyes. "It's a double celebration. They accepted my application for the family medicine residency. I'm in."

"That's fantastic news," he said with a laugh. "Congratulations." He leaned over and kissed her. "Of course, it shouldn't be a surprise. How could they not accept you?"

Trace took an extra sip of his champagne and tried to relax the tense muscles between his shoulder blades. He had made it over one hurdle getting into medical school, but the bigger hurdle was still to come.

The limousine pulled into his dad's new housing development and stopped in front of a two-story house tucked away on a quiet crescent.

Margo threw him a questioning look. The driver opened the door, and Trace stepped out and reached for Margo's hand. He tipped the driver and stood on the sidewalk with Margo as the limo pulled away.

"What do you think?" he asked.

"Of the house?" Margo stared at it. "It's gorgeous. I love the dark brown brick, the black window frames, and the little balcony. I painted a similar one last week, and the layout is spectacular. The architect who designed it is a genius."

"It's Jacob's work."

"Your brother? Wow. Talented family." She grinned.

He tugged her hand. "Let's go inside."

She hesitated a moment, but at the pull, followed his lead. Trace took out a key and opened the door, then stepped back and swept Margo into his arms to carry her over the threshold. Margo laughed and clung to his shoulder. "Don't dislocate your shoulder again," she warned.

Trace kissed her. "You're too light for that."

He set her down inside the door, and Margo looked around. Straight ahead, soft light filled a dining room with a small table set for two. A crisp white tablecloth fell to the floor, and candles surrounded a bouquet of red roses.

Trace followed her gaze. "I have to light the candles. I didn't want to burn the house down before we got here."

Margo glanced at him. "Wise. I'm surprised your dad's letting you use the house. Hasn't it been sold?"

"He was okay with it. Come on, I want to show you something." They took the stairs to the right. "The sitting room is there." He pointed to the area opposite the staircase on the main floor. "The kitchen's behind it. And there are three bedrooms up here."

At the end of the hall, he opened double doors to the master suite and smiled when Margo sighed with pleasure.

A queen-sized bed sat across from a picture window. Flowers tumbled out of vases around the room. The faint perfume of orchids filled the air. Spring tulips, daisies, roses in every color, and vibrant birds of paradise were tucked into vases.

"And through here . . ." Trace said, showing her a sparkling bathroom in white and pale gray marble, a glass shower stall with a rain head and body jets, and a deep tub filled with steamy water and rippling bubbles.

"That looks very inviting," Margo said.

"That's what I thought, too."

Margo reached over and slowly unbuttoned his shirt and slipped it off his shoulders. Then she stepped back and lifted her dress over her head.

Trace's body stirred at the lacy bits of fabric she wore. He shed his pants and stood naked, watching Margo's eyes darken when her gaze roamed over him.

She turned her back to Trace. "Can you help me with the clasp?"

Trace stepped closer, aching to touch, and released the fabric. He slid he hands around her ribcage and cupped the fullness of her breasts in his hands.

He pressed against her, loving the smooth softness of

her skin. "I've heard a thong can be uncomfortable. Maybe I should help you with that."

"Hmmm," Margo hummed.

His hands were busy.

Much later, Margo arched her back and stretched luxuriously. "I could so get used to this," she purred.

Trace, lying on his side on the bed beside her, ran his fingers from her neck, down around the fullness of her breast, and across her belly. "Could you?"

"Absolutely. Sensory overload in a bath full of bubbles, a rough tumble in sateen sheets. You by my side. What's not perfect about that?" She smiled and brushed the side of his face.

Trace stilled and looked at her. He brushed his lips against hers and then reached across to the bedside table. He fished behind the vase of flowers, pulled out a small box, and handed it to her.

Margo's eyes widened, and she sat up. He could see her heart pounding in her chest. She took the box with shaking hands and slowly lifted the lid. She stared at the ring, and then at him.

"I love you, Margo. I can't imagine anything more perfect than you by my side every day. I love your smile." He traced a hand over her lips. "Your heart." He traced a hand over her heart. "I love the way you think." He ran his hands over her curls and brushed away a tear. "I love you, Margo. Will you marry me?"

"Yes." She laughed and wiped the tears impatiently with the back of her hand. "I love you, Trace," she whispered.

His breath caught, and his heart swelled at the words. The sweetest words ever. He took the ring from the box and slid it on her finger. "Perfect fit."

"Yes," Margo said, looking him in the eye. "You're my perfect fit." She laughed and threw her arms around his neck, holding him close. He held her tightly and felt a surge of pleasure.

Now life was complete.

They lit the candles, ate filet mignon, and drank champagne in the dining room. Margo couldn't get enough of the sweet scent of the roses. It had been a magical evening.

She admired the radiant diamond on her finger. She twisted it in the light and watched as it shimmered in a rainbow of color. "I didn't expect this," she said quietly.

"No? I've loved you for a while."

Margo's heart swirled. She paused. "You seemed so," she waved her hand, "distant and quiet after the tournament. I thought I'd lost you."

Trace nodded slowly. "You told me you were going back to medicine."

Margo gave him a puzzled look. "Why did that change things?"

"It meant I had to take a step back until I found out whether I was accepted into medical school. If you were going to practice medicine, you'd need someone far better than me to support you."

"You mean financially? I've been supporting myself financially for a long time."

"No, not financially. Emotionally. You're going to be dealing with a ton of shit, like the examples you gave me, like my interview. You need someone by your side who understands all that, who can say the right things, who gets it."

"Trace." She reached out and interlocked her fingers with his hand resting on the table. "Getting into medical school doesn't change who you are. You're loyal, compassionate, and generous. You already listen and say the right things. You don't need a medical degree for that. It's your voice I want to hear, and your shoulder I want to lean on." She squeezed his hand. "I love you for who you are, not for the letters after your name."

Trace smiled slowly, with love shining in his eyes. "I love you, Margo."

"I love you, too. We're going to have to get to know whoever buys this house. It holds a precious memory. That's good feng shui," Margo said.

Trace laughed. "Do you like it?"

"The house? Yeah. It's gorgeous."

"It's mine." He smiled. "Ours."

"What?"

"I bought it this afternoon. I hoped you'd share it with me." He brought her hand to his lips and gently kissed it. "I figured we'd be here for a while, with me starting medical school, and you starting family medicine." He grinned. "I got a family discount."

Margo laughed, delighted, and reached across the table to kiss him. "There is one thing, though," she said tongue-in-cheek, "that may be a deal breaker."

Trace raised his eyebrows.

"What kind of car do you drive?"

Trace laughed and stood up. "Come with me." He held out his hand, and she followed him past the kitchen and powder room, through the laundry room to a door. He opened the door and nodded for her to take a look.

Margo stuck her head into the garage and burst out laughing. "Of course." She fell into his open arms. "I love you."

CPSIA information can be obtained
at www.ICGtesting.com
Printed in the USA
LVOW04s0250141215
466531LV00007B/12/P